ABOUT THE AUTHOR

When Geoffrey McSkimming was a boy he
found an old motion-picture projector and a tin
containing a dusty film in his grandmother's attic.
He screened the film and was transfixed by
the flickering image of a man in a jaunty pith helmet,
baggy Sahara shorts and special desert sun-spectacles.
The man had an imposing macaw and a clever looking
camel, and Geoffrey McSkimming was mesmerised
by their activities in black-and-white Egypt, Peru,
Greece, Mexico, Sumatra, Turkey, Italy and
other exotic locations.

Years later he discovered the identities of the trio,
and has spent much of his time since then retracing
their footsteps, interviewing surviving members of the
Old Relics Society, and gradually reconstructing these
lost true tales which have become the enormously
successful Cairo Jim chronicles.

Geoffrey McSkimming wrote *Cairo Jim Amidst
the Petticoats of Artemis* after travelling through Turkey,
visiting the places explored by Cairo Jim, Doris
the macaw and Brenda the Wonder Camel, and feeling
the strange presence of the Belligerent Serpent of
Antiocheia in the ground beneath his feet…

For Belinda,
who saw the egg motifs with me in Turkey

First published in Great Britain 2007 by Walker Books Ltd
87 Vauxhall Walk, London SE11 5HJ

2 4 6 8 10 9 7 5 3 1

Text © 2000 Geoffrey McSkimming
Cover illustration © 2007 Walker Books Ltd

This book has been typeset in Plantin

Printed in Great Britain by
Cox & Wyman Ltd, Reading, Berkshire

British Library Cataloguing in Publication Data:
a catalogue record for this book is available from the British Library.

ISBN 978-1-4063-0598-2

www.walkerbooks.co.uk

CAIRO JIM

AMIDST THE PETTICOATS OF ARTEMIS

A Turkish Tale of Treachery

GEOFFREY McSKIMMING

WALKER
BOOKS

▲▲▲▲▲ CONTENTS ▲▲▲▲▲

The store-room in the ruins of the Temple of Domitian
at Ephesus – where the first relic was found.
Photograph taken by Pyrella Frith before the store-room's destruction.

Part One:

DRUPACEOUS GARMENT

STORMY PURSUIT

THE RAIN HAMMERED DOWN on the ancient ruins of Ephesus as though all the heavens above Turkey had burst wide and savagely open.

Great rivers of water swept down the pathways and roadways where once, thousands of years ago, men and women, children and animals had moved through their daily lives.

Blinding flashes of lightning lit up the faces of long-forgotten, crumbling statues as they watched over their storm-lashed city.

Deafening bursts of thunder crashed and then rolled above what remained of the Library of Celsus, the most wonderful of the ruins.

The wind whipped the raindrops into a stinging frenzy through the streets and the broken shells of buildings, abandoned this dark and violent night by the throngs of tourists who were regular visitors in daylight hours.

Through all of this whirling turbulence, through all of this cracking-open of the world, through all of this storm to end all storms, came the slapping sound of fat shoes running on the cobblestones of Curetes Street.

"Arrr! Arrr! Arrr! Arrr! Hurry, you drenched, dimwitted disaster! They're coming closer!"

"Rark!" shrieked Desdemona the raven, battling against the stinging water and repellent wind. "I'm flying as fast as I can!"

"Well move FASTER! Arrrr!" Neptune Flannel-bottom Bone slipped on a rough patch of stones and went bouncing and sprawling into a wall. He rolled over, picked himself up, and kept running, rivulets of water flowing down from his fez and into his eyes.

Only fifty metres behind him, watery torchbeams glowed through the wall of rain. Distant voices – voices belonging to men from the Kusadasi Branch of the Antiquities Squad – shouted urgently above the noise of the storm:

"Ahead, ahead!"

"I see him, there, by the Temple of Hadrian!"

"There he is, up near the Trajan Fountain!"

"No, no, he is approaching the Herakles Gate!"

"I knew I shouldn't have worn these pants tonight!"

"Hurry, men, hurry!"

"Desdemona," Bone hissed urgently as he splashed and skidded up the slippery street, "start swooping about! Go high, then low, then high again! Distract the torchlight from me!"

"That'd take an awful lot of distraction," the raven croaked into the rain. "There's an awful lot of you to—"

"DO IT!"

"Crark!" She obeyed, shooting up against the downpour, and then backwards and forwards, swooping low and rising again, all along the storm-barraged street.

"That's it." The fleshy, obese figure of Bone paused for an instant, his eyes darting left and right, trying to find the best escape route. "Somewhere unremarkable," he muttered desperately to himself. "Somewhere they won't think to search..."

"Look!" cried one of the men from the Antiquities Squad. *"That shadow!"*

"What is it?" shouted another.

"Creerrraaarrrrrkkkkk!" howled Desdemona, as the hundreds of fleas concealed in her feathers chomped into her tough, bitter flesh.

"A bat?"

"No, a ghost! A ghost from the ancient past!"

"Fools! It's a bird – a huge, black bird!"

"Ooh, I hate it when pants ride up like this!"

"Ignore the bird, we want the man!"

The crazed Bone heard their footsteps echoing loudly in his direction, and, swivelling about, he saw their beams shafting around the corner, glinting off the wet columns of the Memmius Monument. He turned and looked wildly about the ruins.

CRRRAAAAAAAAAAAAAAACCCCCCCCCCKK-KKKKKKKKKKKK!

A thunderclap savage enough to proclaim the destruction of the skies ripped through Ephesus, and was followed, an instant later, by a lightning strike that seemed to light up the whole world.

And, in that blaze of eye-burning light, Bone saw his route: the ruins of the Temple of Domitian.

"Thank you, Mother!" Taking a huge breath, he left the cobblestoned street and ran and skidded along the muddy, unpaved pathway.

The rain pelted harder as he splashed towards the two standing columns of the Temple and the foundation stones that lay strewn on the ground.

"Where is he? Where has he gone?"

The lights of the Antiquities Squad became still as the men stopped running. Then the beams began waving all across the rain-sodden site.

"Arrr," gasped Bone, clumping along in puddles the size of small swimming pools. His plus-fours trousers were sopping wet, especially around his countryside of a bottom, and the spats that covered his shoes resembled two vast and sloppy mudpies.

His eyes searched through the debris of the once-mighty Temple, sleering up to the two remaining statues mounted high on the columns. As the raindrops cascaded down their marble faces, they seemed to be looking upon him scornfully and hopelessly.

"You wretched frozen failures from the dust-heap of History," he snarled at them, and still they regarded him in the same dismissive manner.

"Maybe," suggested one of the Antiquities Squad men, *"he went to the Temple of Domitian?"*

"No, see, there are no footprints in the mud!"

"There is hardly any mud to leave footprints in – it's turning into a lake over there!"

"Ooooh! So help me, I'll murder the man who made these pants!"

"Where, where, where?" Bone puffed his way to the rear of the columns. Here was a series of vaulted enclosures, set into the hillside. A lightning strike from over the hills revealed that the enclosures were too shallow to hide in – one flash from a torch and he would be lit up like a rabbit in a burrow.

"Craaaark!" Desdemona swooped in by his side, her feathers oozing rainwater. "Hurry, hurry, hurry, they're coming this way!"

CRRRAAAAAAAAAAAAAAACCCCCCCCCCKK-KKKKKKKKKKKKK!

This thunderclap was even louder than the last, and Bone's eardrums almost exploded from the blast.

The lightning shot down, spearing through a tree not ten metres away, with a sound that could have ripped through time itself.

Desdemona's blood-red eyeballs throbbed so hard they almost leapt out of her skull.

But in the instant of harsh, brutal exposure, Bone saw the place to go – off to the right, a streaming muddy trail rose up into the hillside. Built into the side of the hill was a small marble doorframe, sur-rounded by overgrown weeds and ivy and a few fallen marble slabs, and topped with a semicircular wall of ancient bricks. On the other side of the door-frame, inside the hill itself, was the equivalent of a human-made cave.

"Quick, bird, follow me, and use those wings of yours to be useful for once! Wipe out my footprints on the way into that hill!"

Desdemona was about to protest, but then she saw the lights from the Squad bobbing over the huge foundation stones as they came closer. She began hopping along the mud, thrashing her wings over every chubby footprint he left.

"Quick, in here!" He squeezed himself through the doorway and, grabbing her by the throatfeathers, yanked her inside too. Silently they groped their way up the dark floor, until they were ensconced deep in the womb of the hill.

Out by the two columns, the Antiquities Squad stopped.

"Doesn't look like he came this way."

"There'd be footprints if he had."

"I bet he kept going up Curetes Street. Let's go back there, and be quick about it!"

"Now I know how a shish kebab feels!"

Deep within their cave-like seclusion, Neptune Bone and Desdemona listened as the men of the Kusadasi Branch of the Antiquities Squad sloshed off into the deluge.

"Arrrr," grunted the large man, settling himself on a dry patch of dirt and taking off his lemon-toned fez with the peach-fuzz-coloured tassel. "See, Desdemona? I told you we'd be all right."

The raven wrung out the feathers above her left leg,

squirting an arc of water against the earth wall. "Sheesh, that was close!"

"Mmmm." He took his silver cigar-lighter and two stumpy candles from the pockets of his emerald-green waistcoat. "But we've eluded them yet again, haven't we?"

"Only just. It'll take me three weeks to dry out after all this!"

There was a small *whoooosh*, and the flame from the cigar-lighter ignited the candles. Bone picked up one of the candles (being careful not to hold it beneath any of the small drips that were leaking through from the ground above) and moved the light around their new abode.

"Hmmm," he hmmmed. "Must've once been part of the Temple of Domitian. Not very ornate – the walls are rougher than your tongue. They don't appear to have even been plastered or decorated. Probably just a store-room or something. Those Antiquities Squad goons wouldn't even know it's here."

"What a way to spend my days," whined Desdemona. "Running all over the world, escaping from the Antiquities Squad, hiding from the International Police and that fanatical debt collector from your tailor in Port Moresby." She pecked six fleas from her underwing and crunched them in her beak. "I should've listened to Mother. Should've found meself a suitably gloomy poet and settled down with him, swooping into his study regularly whenever there was a full moon. *That's* the life I should be leading. Nevermore, nevermore, nevermore! Crark!"

"Enshut your beak. You forget, you ridiculous riot of rancidity, that you are privileged to be in the constant presence of greatness. I have come up with more plans of Absolute Brilliance than any other man you are ever likely to encounter."

"And they've all failed miserably."

"They have had *setbacks*. All Geniuses such as what I am have had setbacks. It's part of the character-building process of being a Genius."

"It's part of the reason for me getting migraines all the time." Her red eyes were throbbing even more harshly than usual. "And I think I feel one comin' on right now."

"You do not have to worry, bird. Not when you're with me. As my immediate history should tell you, the prospect of unimaginably great opportunity frequently throws itself across my path."

"Oh, brother!" She shook the water out of her wings. "The only thing that crosses *your* path is the god of hot air!"

"Enshut your beak before I enshut it for you."

"What with? A blast of verbosity?"

He picked up a clod of earth and lobbed it at her head. It struck her above the eyebrowfeathers and she gave a small wail.

Bone took out his cigar case and opened it. Inside, his three Belch of Brouhaha cigars were sodden and mushy. "Arrrr," he grimaced, removing them and placing them on a low dirt ledge where they could dry out.

"'Twas a pity our Montgolfier balloon came down the way it did," he grumbled, making himself as comfortable as he could against the wall. "I suspect some of those bullets from the Egyptian Antiquities Squad pierced the balloon when we took off from Giza yesterday."

"One way to get rid of too much hot air," thought Desdemona, but she said nothing, for fear of another wayward earth-clod missile.

"But at least we're safe now. And dry. There are only a few small drips to contend with in here, and tomorrow the world will be my oyster once more. Arrrr."

"I know where there's an *enormous* drip to contend with," muttered Desdemona. "And he's not going away in a hurry."

Bone pulled out his gold fob-watch and examined the dial. "Three-thirty-three in the morning," he announced. "Time for some shut-eye. Wake me at eleven, Desdemona, and not before. And don't drool in my ear to awaken me. A simple, 'Oh, my brilliant Captain, it is eleven o'clock and the world is your oyster' will do."

Ever heard of an alarm clock? she thought.

"And, heavens to the Goddess Betsy, try not to belch in your sleep tonight."

With a prune-smelling puff, he blew out the candles, as the raven rolled her eyeballs and tried to find a warm place to roost. Outside, the rain continued to hammer down, as if tomorrow would never come...

2

THE TURNING UP OF THINGS

BECAUSE COUNTING and the telling of time were two things she wasn't very good at, Desdemona promptly woke Neptune Bone at four-thirty in the afternoon. She managed this feat by perching on his shoulder and dripping a long, slimy trail of ravendrool slowly into his left ear.

The fleshy man opened one eye and then the other. He looked up at the ceiling of their cave-like abode to see if the rain was dripping in on him. Then he caught a whiff of Desdemona's natural fragrance – a smell that only settles on a bird when it hasn't cleaned itself for at least two months.

"Arrrrrr!" He swatted her fiercely off his shoulder, and she fluttered onto a mound of dirt and mud in the corner.

"Wakey, wakey, oh mountain of snoringness," she croaked.

With a loud grunt, he sat upright and wiggled a fat finger about in his ear hole. "You disgusting, grotty, talon-cursed idiot!"

"All part of the service," she rasped, before pecking at a flea on her wing.

"What time is it?" He pulled out his fob-watch,

looked at it and frowned. "Trust me to rely on a numerically challenged twerp."

"It's still raining out there," Desdemona informed him. "Hasn't let up all night. I should know – didn't get a winkling of sleep, on accounta this aching head of mine. Oooh. Feels like I've got a line-dancing marathon goin' on in there!"

Bone stretched his arms wide and yawned. "Maybe all the rain's a good thing. It would have kept lots of those trampling, ignorant tourists away for the day."

"None of 'em came near the door of our new 'home', I'm here ta tell ya." She scowled. "As if this headache wasn't enough, I kept havin' these dreams. Kept seein' this big eye, opening and closing in the ground. Kept dreamin' of snakes. Sheesh!"

Bone took up one of the candle stubs and lit it; despite the hour of the day, the place inside the hill was still smothered by a rich, deep gloom, and all he could see of the bird was the occasional glint of her red eyes whenever they throbbed silently.

"Wretched tourists," he muttered, lighting the other candle stub. Carefully he placed the two flames onto the dirt ledge by his shoulder.

"Crark. How long are we gonna be stuck here? Every time we have to run away from one of your doomed hare-brained schemes, we always have to hide in some dirty, leaking hole somewhere. Sheesh. I haven't eaten since I don't know when – not counting all these fleas I have to gobble before I end up lookin' like a pin-cushion. If I don't get my beak into some tinned Japanese seaweed soon, I'll—"

"Look!"

"—go outta my mind, I just know—"

"Shut up and look!"

"Eh?" She closed her beak and stared at him.

The eyes of Neptune Bone were wide, and his hairy eyebrows (which resembled two plump and overfed caterpillars) had crept up his broad forehead, as if they intended to say hello to his greasy hairline.

"What's got you so startled?" asked Desdemona.

His eyebrows lowered a fraction, and his eyes started to return to their natural slitty state. He extended a chubby forefinger. "Look at that upon which you are perched!"

She lowered her beak and moved her head around. "So? A big pile of moist dirt." She lifted a leg and waggled her claws about. "Verging on mud in some bits. So what?"

"It's a *new* mound, Desdemona!"

"Eh?"

"It wasn't there this morning, when we crawled in here. See?" He pointed to a cavity in the hill behind her. "All this rain has washed it down, out of the wall!"

"Oh, how *fantastic*! What a *marvellous* thing! This has gotta be the biggest discovery since Captain Cook took a wrong turn at Tahiti! I can just see the headlines: 'Manicured Maniac Finds Magnificent Mound of Mud'. The world'll *really* sit up and take notice, I'm sure."

"ENSHUT YOURSELF!" He hurled a hardened clod of mud at her belly.

"Oooof! Okay, okay, okay, I'm enshutted."

"Do you think that I would allow myself to become excited by an unexpected dumping of mud and dirt? Oh, no, no, no, there's more to it. More that you haven't bothered to see." He crawled over to her. "Look at this!"

She glared at the bit of mound that he was rubbing his hands over, and her beak dropped open. "Well pickle my eyeballs!"

"Arrrr," said Neptune Bone.

His hands were caressing the edge of something that was jutting out from the mound: a muddy, dirt-encrusted edge that glinted here and there the colour of dull silver.

Bone grabbed Desdemona by her throat and pulled her down. "Help me, bird. Use that beak of yours to gouge out some of this dirt and gunk. Let's see what we have."

"What about you? You've got fingers!"

"Gouge!" He shoved her razor-sharp beak close to the edge of the object. She took a gulp of air, and began to poke and scrape.

"That's it ... keep gouging ... that's the way."

"There," she spat after two minutes. "Is that enough?"

"For the moment, yes."

"What is it?"

"Hmmm. Looks like a lid. Hard to tell, until we dig it out. Arrr, Desdemona! See the pattern!"

All along the top of the edge of the lid was a raised design of small, egg-shaped motifs, each egg-shape exactly the same as the one next to it.

Bone rubbed mud from one of the egg-shapes, and smelled his finger. His eyes filled with creeping lust. "Au. Au, Au, Au!"

"Eh you, what?"

"Not 'eh you', *Au*! The chemical symbol for gold," he whispered. "These eggy things are all made of gold! Arrrrr!"

Desdemona threw back her head and cackled.

"Stop that cackling, you doubting dumdum. You have a little pressing excavation ahead of you."

For the next half an hour, Desdemona used her beak and talons to break up the dirt and mud that encased the silver, gold-egged object. The earth was awful in her mouth, and squelchy between her claws, but she continued without argument; this might be something that humans called 'a turn up for the books'. Something that may change the circumstances for her and Bone. Something that would mean she could have her tinned Japanese seaweed again soon.

Throughout her digging and clearing, Bone sat in the corner, smoking one of his (dried) Belch of Brouhaha cigars and watching her eagerly.

"Pphhhsssssttt," she spat at last. "There. Now you should be able to lever it out."

Bone crawled over and gripped the top sides of the

silver object. There was still a little mud and dirt at each end, but the raven had exposed all of the front and a section of the top surface. He took a big breath and began to rock and twist the object, first to the right, then to the left. Then to the right again.

"That's it," encouraged Desdemona. "More, more, more. It's starting to move!"

"Arrrr," puffed Bone, the sweat running down into his stubbly beard.

He kept twisting and rocking the mass of silver and gold, and each time, it moved a little more and became looser.

"Nearly there," said Desdemona.

"One last…" He gave a mighty jerk to the left, and the object – and what was left of the mud surrounding it – came free, falling out onto Bone's lap, and knocking him backwards.

"Ooofff!"

"How the mighty have fallen. Ha-crark-har!"

"Quick, get this thing off me!"

She pushed it to the floor, and Bone sat up. "A casket," he whispered.

"A *silver and gold* casket," croaked Desdemona.

It wasn't a very large casket – only about thirty centimetres long, twenty centimetres broad, and twenty centimetres high. Its lid was domed, with straight edges where it joined the box itself, and halfway along the lid was a small square lock, with a round hole in the centre. All around every edge, and around the lock, the pattern of gold egg-shapes was repeated. Apart from this, there was no other sign of decoration, or inscription, or ornament.

Bone took one of the candles and moved its flame over the casket. "Hmmm. I reckon this might've been put in here for safekeeping. Might've been used in the Temple of Domitian out there. Obviously they forgot all about it, way back when."

"What's it worth? What's it worth?"

"A good deal, I should think. Should fetch us a pretty price on the black market somewhere."

"Hey, maybe there's something inside!"

Bone looked at her, startled.

"Pardon me," he said, in mock surprise. "Did I hear a little tad of intelligence descend into your skull?"

"Eh?"

"That's the first smart thing you've said," he told her.

"Thank you very much." She wasn't sure if that was a compliment or an insult.

"Let's see if there *is* anything within."

He reached into his pocket and withdrew an oversized bobby-pin (his mother had told him, long ago, never to leave home without one). This he shoved into the hole in the casket's lock.

"Seems to be something in this lock." He jiggled the bobby-pin. "Dirt, I'd say. This thing has probably been locked for thousands of years."

Desdemona's eyes became redder as she watched.

"Just a bit more ... there!"

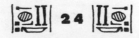

With a loud *click*, he turned the bobby-pin and took it out.

Desdemona's breathing grew raspier.

He gripped the front edges of the lid and tried to push it up.

"Stuck," he said.

"Try again," she urged.

He put his huge weight behind the effort this time, and tried to lift once more.

"Won't budge," he puffed, the veins standing out in his neck.

"Don't give up! Go on, go on, go on!"

Clenching his teeth, he had another go. His knuckles turned white, his eyebrows ran with sweat, his thighs trembled.

"It's useless," he sighed, collapsing back onto the earth floor.

"Stupid casket," sneered the raven. She hopped up onto the lid and gave it a sharp *thwaaackkk* with her beak.

The lid sprang open, throwing her into the mound of mud behind.

"Arrr." Bone crept forward, the candle stub between his fingers.

Desdemona squelched her wings and hop-fluttered around to his side.

Together they peered into the time-locked casket, as the candle's flame danced dazzlingly off the untarnished silver surface inside.

When he saw what was lying at the bottom, Bone's eyes filled with malevolent, unsurpassed delight, and his eyebrows shot up, like rockets, to his hairline.

In the Library of the Old Relics Society in Cairo, Gerald Perry Esquire had immersed himself in a very big book about hedgehogs.

His old, possum-like eyes twinkled in the late afternoon sunlight as he turned page after page. He had never had a burning, or even a passing, interest in hedgehogs; he had just found the book an hour earlier, lying by a statue of Pharaoh Sesostris I, down in the statue gallery on the lower floor. He had thought it was too nice a book to leave lying there.

He was in the middle of the South American Hedgehogs bit when Cairo Jim – that well-known archaeologist and little-known poet – led Brenda the Wonder Camel into the vast library. Doris the macaw sat on Jim's shoulder, flexing herself impatiently up and down.

"Afternoon, Perry," said Jim, in his soft and well-modulated voice.

"D'you know," said Perry, reading from the page before him, "that there's a hedgehog in Venezuela that's got eyes in its..." He frowned and quickly shut the book. "Never mind about that, it's really not important."

He rose from his chair and shook Jim's hand. "Hello,

you clever three. I s'pose you've finished your work on the Giza plateau?"*

Cairo Jim took off his pith helmet and special desert sun-spectacles. "We have."

"Rark." Doris flexed her beautiful yellow and blue wings. "And now," she squawked, flexing herself more energetically, "we've come to say goodbye for the time being. Rerk. We're going home!"

"Back to the Valley of the Kings," smiled Jim.

"Quuaaaooo," snorted Brenda happily, for she had missed their home campsite dearly.

"And you all deserve it," Perry grinned. "I'm sad to see you all go, but I'll catch up with you very soon. There are two things in my life I'm certain about: that osnaburg underpants make me itch, and that my path and your paths will cross regularly. After all, with all my money, I have to fund *someone's* excavations. Right?"

"Too right," said Jim.

"Rerark, c'mon, Jim, the sooner we get there, the sooner we can go to Mrs Amun-Ra's Tea Rooms and—"

But she was interrupted by a bold voice from beyond the doorway: "It will be quite some time before the three of you can taste the delicacies of Mrs Amun-Ra. There is trouble afoot in Turkey!"

---

* See *Cairo Jim and the Secret Sepulchre of the Sphinx – A Tale of Incalculable Inversion*

3

A REQUEST FROM MELTEM BOTTNOFF

JIM, DORIS, BRENDA and Perry turned their heads at the sudden vocal intrusion.

"Good afternoon," said the petite, dark-haired woman in the doorway. She entered the library, striding in an I'm-here-on-business sort of way, the trousers of her smartly tailored, lime-green suit swishing briskly through the silence.

"Good afternoon," said Perry. "Er..."

"Let me introduce myself," she said, reaching into her blazer pocket and pulling out a small silver badge in an open leather wallet. This she flashed quickly. "I am Meltem Bottnoff, Senior Retriever of Ancientness with the Istanbul Branch of the Antiquities Squad."

"Pleased to meet you," Cairo Jim said, extending his hand. "I'm—"

"I know who you are, Cairo Jim." She shook his hand, her deep brown eyes lighting up for an instant. "There is not an Antiquities Squad Officer the world over who would not know of *you*."

Jim blushed, and Doris stretched her wings. "Rerk, c'mon, Jim. Brenda and I are itching to get back to camp!"

"And you," said Meltem Bottnoff, addressing the

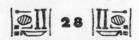

28

macaw, "can be none other than the noble bird, Doris. I have been following your achievements for many years in the newspapers."

"Coo," cooed Doris.

"And the third member of importance." Meltem reached across and gently stroked Brenda's snout. "Brenda the Wonder Camel, the most gifted Bactrian in all the lands."

"Quaaaooo." Brenda's long eyelashes fluttered modestly.

"Well, you certainly know of m'colleagues," Gerald Perry said.

"And I know of *you*, Mr Perry." Meltem extended her hand to him, and he shook it, his eyes twinkling and his moustache going all bristly.

"Ah," she said, noticing the book on his chair. "You have been reading about hedgehogs? Did you know that there is a species of hedgehog in Venezuela that has its eyes in its—"

"Er, yes, yes," Perry said quickly. "Was just reading about it."

"Yes, indeed, Mr Perry," she smiled, "I know of you. It is not a secret that without the generous support of Gerald Perry Esquire, Cairo Jim and his friends would often be in hot water. Would they not?"

"Well, er, I wouldn't go so far as *that*," stammered Perry, captivated by her smile. "Tepid sometimes, perhaps, but Jim's pretty resourceful, never doubt that."

"I would never doubt that," she answered, shifting

her smile so that it fell (like a sunbeam, Perry thought) onto Cairo Jim.

"Well, it's been very nice to meet you, Senior Retriever Bottnoff," Jim said as Doris jerked up and down. "But if you'll excuse us, we have to be getting back to our campsite in the Valley of the Kings. We've been away for a long time, and—"

"I'm afraid that time will become *longer*," she interrupted. "And you must call me Meltem, please."

"Rark!" Doris screeched.

"Longer?" asked Jim.

"Let us sit, if we may."

"By all means," Perry said, gesturing towards a group of plump leather armchairs nearby. He and Meltem sat down. Reluctantly, Jim, Doris and Brenda joined them.

Meltem crossed her legs and undid her lime-green blazer. As she did so, Jim glimpsed a tiny, black pistol in a shoulder-holster under the blazer. "I know that what I am about to ask you will not be very welcome," she said gravely as she patted her lustrous black hair, which was tied in a tight bun at the back of her head.

"We're listening," Jim said. "Aren't we, gang?"

"Mm-hmm," said Doris.

"Quaaoo," snorted Brenda.

"Oh, yes indeedy," said Perry in a dreamy sort of voice as he watched the sunlight shining on Meltem's bun.

"I know how eager you all are to return to the Valley of the Kings. Our papers in Turkey have carried the stories of your latest discovery at Giza, and the awful things that happened there for you. But we need your help, Jim, Doris and Brenda, now more than ever before!"

"How?" Jim fiddled with the brim of his pith helmet in his lap. "To do what?"

"To finally apprehend and lock away that most devious, underhanded and fashion-senseless man, Captain Neptune Flannelbottom Bone."

"RAAAAARRRRRKKKKKK!" Doris let fly with a crescendo of fury at the sound of his name. "The cad! The overblown, evil brute! He almost ruined Jim over the last few months! That rapscallion! That bloated dreg of naughtiness! That baby hippopotamus lookalike!"

Jim patted her crest. "Steady on, my dear. He didn't destroy us in the end, did he?"

"He came close. Rark!"

"And that," said Meltem, "is one of the reasons why we should try and find him, as quickly as possible. As you know better than anyone else, Cairo Jim, he wreaks havoc wherever he goes: archaeological destruction, major vandalism, gross distortion of the truth and the total abuse and manipulation of History – not to mention random acts of graffiti and running naked in the streets."

"She's right, Jim," nodded Perry, still watching the sun dancing about on her hair. "He has to be caught."

Jim frowned. "So, Ms Bottnoff—"

"Meltem," she corrected.

"Meltem," whispered Perry to himself.

"So, Meltem, do you and your associates know where Bone *is*?"

"This is what brings me to the Old Relics Society," she answered. "Two days ago, there was a dreadful storm over south-western Turkey. Ephesus, to be exact. The rains lashed the ancient buildings and monuments with the ferocity of a small tornado. After the storm had passed, after it had blown away into the Mediterranean, the remnants of a hot-air balloon were found scattered around the Harbour Street precinct of Ephesus."

"Ephesus!" breathed Jim. "One of the greatest ancient cities ever! I haven't been there for years."

"A hot-air balloon," breathed Doris.

"Meltem," breathed Perry, without realising it.

Brenda had a thought – a thought which travelled from her Wonder Camel brain telepathically into the library. *"Was this balloon a Montgolfier?"*

The thought entered Doris's head. "Was this balloon a Montgolfier?" she asked.

Meltem pulled out a tiny notebook from her blouse pocket – again Jim saw the small pistol in her holster. "Yes," she nodded, consulting the notebook. "It *was* a Montgolfier. Had the name 'Persephone' painted on what remained of the basket."

"Jocelyn's!" exclaimed Jim.

Meltem put the notebook away. "Jocelyn?"

"Cairo Jim's 'good friend'," explained Perry. "She's a Flight Attendant with Valkyrian Airways."

"Oh," said Meltem, crossing her legs the other way.

"Yes," Jim said. "She was helping us for a while on the dig. She rented Persephone when she came. She's into aeronautics in a big way, is Joss."

Meltem adjusted her bun and said nothing, while Doris rolled her eyes.

"It was in Persephone that Neptune Bone escaped."

"He stole it, the thieving scumhead!" screeched Doris.

"Ah!" Meltem clasped her hands about her upper-most kneecap. "We thought as much! Now we *know* that it was he who crash-landed at Ephesus."

"So where d'you think the scoundrel is?" Perry asked, surveying Meltem's hands for any rings. (He saw none.)

"At this point in time, we do not know. But, Cairo Jim, Doris and Brenda, I am here, on behalf of the entire Antiquities Squad, to request you to come to Turkey and help us find him."

"Come to Turkey?" Jim asked.

"But why us?" Doris said, fluttering her wingtips. "What makes you think *we* could find him?"

"Because the three of you know, better than anyone else, how this deranged man's mind works." Meltem leaned forward and spoke more urgently. "You have encountered him and that felonious raven of his more regularly than anyone else. If there are any who can claim to know how this extraordinary man thinks and acts, and what deeds he is likely to plot, it will be Cairo

Jim, Doris and Brenda the Wonder Camel."

"She's got a few good points there," Brenda thought, and it travelled into Perry's head.

"She's got a few good points there," Perry said enthusiastically, wiggling his eyebrows.

"Please help us," Meltem implored. "You will have every convenience at your disposal that the Antiquities Squad can provide. And I would be most happy" – her eyes met Cairo Jim's as she said this – "indeed, most *honoured,* to accompany you in your search, and to assist you whenever possible, with anything you might require."

Perry's jaw dropped. "D'you hear that, Jim? She'll come with us. Oh, this is even more exciting than the time I was chosen to escort Gina Lollobrigida to the World Piglet Squealing Championships, way back in—"

"I'm sorry, Mr Perry, but my invitation only extends to Cairo Jim, Doris and Brenda."

"Eh?"

"Meltem's right," said Jim. "We do know Bone's ways better than anyone else." He patted Perry on the shoulder. "And that includes you, my friend."

Gerald Perry rubbed his moustache this way and that. "No doubting it," he said, trying to hide his disappointment at not being included. "Anyway, I've lots to do here ... we're opening up three new take-away pigeon restaurants next month, and I'll be running round like a headless ibis." He winked at Meltem. "A little sideline of m' business interests, Meltem."

She smiled at him, and his heart jumped.

Jim lifted Doris off his shoulder and placed her gently on the Wonder Camel's fore hump. "I hardly need say this," he said to them both, "but there are more pressing things ahead for us than returning home. At least for the time being."

Doris puffed out her chestfeathers. "Of course there are!" she squawked. "If we can finally put a stop to Bone's monumentally wicked shenanigans, then the world of archaeology and History and all things modern will be a far, far better place."

"And then we can all get some sleep," thought Brenda.

"And then we can all get some sleep," blurted Perry. He blinked suddenly. "Now why on earth did I say that?"

Meltem stood. "So, let us waste no more time. The Antiquities Squad has a light aircraft waiting at Cairo Aerodrome, ready to take us directly to Ephesus. We have customised the rear seating section for you, Brenda, so your journey will not be too uncomfortable."

"Quaaaooo," came Brenda's snort of thanks.

Doris blinked. "'Towards Ephesus turn our blown sails'," she quoted from *Pericles* by William Shakespeare.

"To Turkey," Meltem said loudly.

"To Turkey," repeated Jim of Cairo, putting on his pith helmet and special desert sun-spectacles. "And may we put an end to the career of that wretched maniac."

THE TRAIL OF TREACHERY

LATE THAT NIGHT, while Jim, Doris, Brenda and Meltem were flying north-east towards Ephesus, Neptune Flannelbottom Bone and Desdemona emerged from the cave-like chamber at the rear of the Temple of Domitian.

"Arrr," he breathed, stretching his flabby arms wide. "Out into the world again!"

"What if those Antiquities Squad goons are still about? What if there're guards watching for us?"

Bone picked up the silver casket and wedged it under his arm. "Harrr! This is Turkey, Desdemona. One thing we don't have to worry about in this country is the presence of guards at ancient sites!"

The raven chuckled, her eyes throbbing brightly.

"Now, follow me. You have some work to do."

"Eh? Where're we going?"

"To Istanbul, you eternally enduring effluence."

"Istanbul?"

He took a cigar out of his waistcoat pocket, bit off the end, spat it onto the ground, threw the cigar's paper band onto the ground as well, and lit the cigar. "Istanbul. What they used to call 'Constantinople'."

"And how in the name of Zasu Pitts do you suppose

we're gonna get there?" She addressed him as if he were a very stupid slug. "Shut our eyes and jump through time, space and the general cosmos?"

"Sarcasm does not suit you, bird. Nor, in fact, does life, but we won't do anything to change that for the time being. I have need of your services in order for us to get to Istanbul."

She looked at him warily. "It doesn't involve *jelly* again, does it?"

"Come! The unstoppable course of History beckons me to stamp my greatness upon it once more."

He turned and sauntered self-importantly through the broken columns and back onto the cobblestoned Curetes Street. Desdemona raised her wings and flew alongside him.

Silently they moved along the street, their shadows seeping across the columns and walls, melting over the statues and doorways. The moonlight shimmered palely against the ancient marble architecture.

Soon Bone came to a shuttered souvenir kiosk, near the entrance of the Library of Celsus. Here he stopped, and placed the casket gently on the ground.

"What's the hold-up?" croaked Desdemona, swooping down to land on his shoulder. "You wanna buy a nice little key-chain with a plastic statue on it?"

He puffed cigar smoke into her eyes. "Here is where we will gather our means of persuasion," he hissed.

"Eh? What poppycock dost thou spout?"

"Quick, you grot-filled harpy, go and snap that

padlock off the kiosk door. Put that beak of yours to some use."

She blinked the smoke from her eyeballs, gave him a look that was part hatred and part curiosity, and then fluttered across to the padlock.

With three savage whacks, her beak smashed the lock. It fell to the ground with a heavy thud.

"Now open the door," Bone commanded.

Edging her beak into the opening, she levered the wooden door open. The hinges gave a long, fingernails-on-the-blackboard screech. Desdemona's eyes throbbed harder at the sound, and the fleas in her feathers bit her more ferociously as the high-pitched noise upset their sensibilities.

"Now, hop aside and let me in there."

As she furiously picked and pecked at the fleas, Bone slunk into the kiosk. After a few minutes of rummaging, he emerged with a bundle of flat posters under his arm and a handful of cigars.

"Got 'em," he whispered. He pocketed the cigars, picked up the casket, and headed off towards the exit gates.

"Hey, wait for me!" Desdemona gave an enormous shake – a few hundred fleas were dislodged by this, and they fell off in all directions – and she flew after him.

"So," she croaked close by his ear as they approached the gate, "whaddya want with them posters?"

"These are going to assist us to obtain a vehicle to get to Istanbul."

"Eh? How? What's on 'em?"

"Time shall reveal all," he answered, kicking the gate open and striding out of the ancient site.

Puzzled, she followed.

After walking for fifteen minutes down a deserted, single-lane road that wound through an overgrown hill, they arrived at a bigger road – one that had four lanes and was well lit.

Bone stopped and looked to the left and the right. There was no traffic, and he crossed slowly to the other side.

"So where's this *veehickel* we're gonna get? The only traffic round here is what's passing through my feathers."

"Something will be along soon enough," he answered. "But first, we have a little littering to do." He put the casket down and took a dozen posters from the bundle under his arm. "Here, Desdemona, take these and scatter them across the road. Place them right-side up, so that any motorist may see the image printed on them."

The raven glared at the black-and-white photo of a man in a black tuxedo and many medals. "Who? Who is it?"

"It is Mustafa Kemal Ataturk. The founding father of this nation. These posters are very valuable to the Turkish people, I'll have you know. They are sold just about everywhere, and collected avidly by the population. I bet there's not a single motorist out there who would not stop to pick these up from the roadway."

"So *that's* your game," she said.

"Game? *Game?* No, you gasping gimlet of grime, it is my *plan*. A *Genius* has plans; an *amateur* plays games."

Desdemona burped and looked at him.

"Go on, scatter!" He thrust the posters into her wings and pushed her onto the road. With a hop, skip and many flutterings, she arranged the posters on the tarred surface, propping them up against roadside rocks and folding some of them in such a way that Mustafa Kemal Ataturk would be seen in any passing headlights.

Bone placed the remaining posters around a nearby tree and between the branches of the shrubs that lined the road.

"There," puffed Desdemona when she had finished. "Now what?"

"Now we wait," he purred, blowing an eager plume of cigar smoke into the night. He ran his hands caressingly over the silver casket, tracing the gold egg-shapes on the edges. "And soon History will smile upon us."

There was little traffic that night, so little that it was nearly two hours before Bone and the raven saw the first beam from a car's headlights. But, as Bone had predicted, the driver was a patriotic subject: with an anguished squeal of the brakes, the small car stopped in the middle of the road.

The door flew open, and the driver – an old man with a white, curly moustache – got out. He stared for a few moments, his eyes wide with shock at the sight of the posters strewn across the road. Then he slowly began to pick them up, one by one, making his way down the roadway.

When he was far enough from the car, Bone and Desdemona came out from the bushes. She shot straight into the car, and Bone squeezed himself into the driver's seat. There was a loud slam of the door, and the car reversed, turned around, and skidded off as the horn blared and faded rudely into the night.

Early the next morning, before Ephesus was opened up for tourists and visitors, Meltem Bottnoff stopped at the lower entrance gate.

"This is strange," she said to Cairo Jim, Doris and Brenda. "This gate is meant to be closed."

Doris hopped off Jim's shoulder and flew to the gate. Here she perched on the wire mesh, and rotated herself until she was upside-down. "Looks like this bit's been kicked almost clean through," she observed.

Jim took off his sun-spectacles and looked at the hole in the mesh.

"A foot's done that," thought Brenda. *"A foot in a wide, fat shoe."*

"A foot's done that," Jim said. "A foot in a wide, fat shoe."

"Rark." Doris poked her head through the hole. "It's been kicked out from this side. From inside the grounds of Ephesus. The kicker came out from inside the site."

"Do you think it was Bone, Jim?" Meltem took the

opportunity to look at his un-sun-spectacled eyes. "Is Bone known to be a kicker?"

"I wouldn't put anything past a man who's hellbent on trying to derail the entire history of civilisation as we know it."

"So," urged Doris, "let's go in and see what he's been up to." She jumped onto the top of the damaged gate and flew off into Ephesus.

"Quaaaooo," snorted Brenda, following her small feathered friend.

"They're keen, aren't they?" Meltem said to Cairo Jim.

"Always have been. That's part of the reason why we're such great friends." He put his sun-spectacles back on. "Let's go hunting."

He and Meltem followed the macaw and Wonder Camel past the colossal remains of the Theatre, to where two streets intersected. Jim pointed to the ruins of the street leading off to the south-west. "Harbour Street," he told her. "So called because thousands of years ago, when the landscape was entirely different, there was a—"

"Harbour down there, with a port." Meltem smiled at him. "That was the first place where all the sailors of the ancient world entered Ephesus."

Jim smiled back. "You know your sites, then."

"All part of the job." She pushed back a lock of her dark hair from her forehead. "We'd better keep up with your friends, Cairo Jim, before they lose us." She gestured towards the street in front of them. "Up Marble Road?"

The archaeologist-poet nodded, still smiling.

They had not gone far when Doris let out an ear-splitting screech from the high grasses by the side of the road. "*Reeeeeerrrraaaaarrrrrrkkkkk!* Here's what's left of that Montgolfier balloon!"

Brenda, who had been inspecting the dirt around one of the broken columns that lined the road, lumbered through the grass and wildflowers to where Doris was hopping about on a piece of the balloon's wicker basket.

"Look, Bren, see here? These letters painted on this bit of the basket say "RSEPHO". That's the middle bit of 'Persephone'."

"*Yes, Doris,*" Brenda thought with a gentle snort, "*I can spell too.*"

"That's it, all right." Jim picked up a piece of the silk balloon that had caught on a low, prickly bush.

"As you will see," said Meltem, "bits of the basket are scattered all over the area bordered by the edge of Harbour Street and Marble Road. Most of the debris is in quite large chunks."

"Which suggests," said Jim, "that the balloon didn't *plummet*. If it had crashed down from a great height at a fast speed, the broken pieces would be smashed and pulverised into much smaller bits."

"We at the Antiquities Squad think that the descent was slow, but unavoidable."

"So," Doris blinked, "any passengers might've survived?"

"That is right, Doris. The Antiquities Squad members on duty the night the balloon crashed believe the trespasser they were chasing was the passenger from this craft."

"And where did the chase go?" Jim asked.

"Come," Meltem said, heading back to Marble Road. "We will retrace the route."

They followed her, through the overgrown grass and wildflowers, and up the road. They went in silence, Doris and Brenda (who had never been to Ephesus before) letting their eyes be filled with the sight of all the beautiful ancient ruins; Jim and Meltem keeping their eyes open for any clues.

Jim stopped and crouched by a line of muddy footprints. "These prints," he said to Meltem. "Has anyone been in here this morning? Any guards or tourists?"

Brenda kept walking on ahead.

Meltem shook her head. "No, not yet. We have given special instructions not to open the site today before eleven o'clock. I wanted the four of us to be undisturbed."

Jim ran his index finger through the still-claggy mud in one of the footprints. "Then this has been made during the night."

Doris hopped across to Jim and poked her beak into the muddiness. "This is pointing in the same direction as the smashed gate," she cooed.

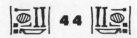

"Does it look like Bone's footprint?" Meltem asked them.

"I'd say so." Jim stood and scratched his forehead under the brim of his pith helmet. "He stole that balloon, and the shoes that made these prints are wide and fat. They'd fit Bone's feet."

"*Quaaaoooo!*" Brenda snorted excitedly from ahead.

"Bren's found something!" Doris screeched. "That's her snort of discovery!"

"There she is," said Meltem. "Near the souvenir kiosk, past the Library of Celsus."

The Wonder Camel was sniffing around the opened door of the kiosk as Jim, Doris and Meltem approached.

Jim picked up the broken padlock. "Been smashed clean off," he said, turning it over in his hands.

Meltem ducked under Brenda's neck and peered into the kiosk. "There is not much disturbed in here, by the look of things."

"Quaooo," Brenda snorted in agreement.

"He must've taken something," frowned Jim. "Come on, let's follow the footprints up Curetes Street. Let's see where he's been."

The sun was rising steadily now, shining through the few greyish-yellow clusters of wispiness that were all that remained of the torrential storm of two days before. The great marble pediments and arches, columns and doorways glistened in the new sunshine as though they were gilded with beads of liquid gold.

Presently Jim stopped, and turned to face the remains of the Temple of Domitian.

"The footprints don't continue past here. Look, right there. They turn off and leave the street. It looks like he ran off into the mud, up near the Temple of Domitian."

Doris squawked and flew off to the Temple, quickly followed by the others.

"Tell me, Meltem," said Jim as they trod carefully through the mud, "is the colossal head and arm of the Emperor Domitian still in the Selcuk Museum?"

"Oh, of course, still on display. They originally came from—"

"The statue that stood on that pedestal over there." Jim smiled at her, and she returned the smile.

"Imagine," she said, "how astonishingly huge the *whole* statue would have been! We think it stood seven metres high!"

"*Quaaaooo.*" Brenda halted and lowered her head to the mud.

"What is it, my lovely?" Jim crouched by her snout and looked at the mud patch.

"Rerk, she's found where the footprints stop completely."

Brenda sniffed the mud, then raised her head and looked to the left and to the right. In neither direction were there any signs of further footprints in the mud.

"He can't just have stopped here," Meltem said. "There's nowhere to hide. The Antiquities Squad would have caught him straight away."

Jim pushed his pith helmet back and scratched his forehead. "Maybe he covered his tracks."

"That'd make sense," Doris cooed. "Knowing Bone."

"Okay, everybody choose a direction and start inspecting. Go slowly, and look everywhere. This is where the felon ran to, all right. Let's find out *exactly* where he went."

They scattered and started searching.

"And what vile madness he's up to *this* time," Jim muttered quietly to himself.

LOOKING FOR ANSWERS

"ARRR, NEXT TIME we need to purloin a car, I think I'll wait for a Bugatti to come along. This contraption is about as comfortable as a bucket of bolts on the back of a hiccupping turtle!"

Bone had been driving the small car non-stop through the night, and the journey had been bumpy at the best of times. At the worst of times, his many rolls of flabbiness had rippled and rolled like an ocean of fat.

Desdemona hopped about on the top edge of the seat next to him. "Are we nearly there yet?" she whined.

He stared at the road ahead and clenched his teeth angrily around his cigar. "Do you have any idea how many times you have asked me that question since we left Ephesus?"

She scratched her pot-belly and thought. "Twice?"

"To you, who have the brain capacity of a stunted marshmallow, it would be twice. For the record, though, you depressingly daft dimwit, you have asked me that same question nine hundred and thirty-four times. 'Are we nearly there yet? Are we nearly there yet? Are we nearly there yet?' I would rather have worms inserted up my nostrils than travel with you."

"Nine hundred and thirty-four? Nah, never. I only

asked it once or twice, when there was a lull in the conversation."

"Hmph. As it so happens, that haze you can see ahead in the early morning light is coming from the outer suburbs of Istanbul. We are getting closer to our destination."

"Why are we coming here, anyway?" She hopped off the back of the seat and down onto the casket. "What's Istanbul got to do with what's in here?"

He steered the car around a minor car crash ahead and his eyes glinted. "If the artefact in that casket is what I think it might be, then I shall have the world at my command in such a way as not even *I* had ever imagined!"

"What? Whaddya reckon's in here?"

"I have an *idea* what it is, but I need my idea to be confirmed. That is why we are coming to Istanbul. We are going to pay a visit to one of my old professors from Archaeology School, who happens to be an expert on early Anatolian and Ephesian history."

"Who? Who is he?"

"Hieronymous von Nozzel."

"Never heard of him."

"That hardly surprises me, you ignorant item of ickiness. The only name *you'd* know is the manufacturer of that dreadful tinned seaweed you love so much."

"Uppiobummoh!"

"What did you say to me?" His beard and moustache bristled, and the fingers on his right hand flexed, ready to wrap around her throat.

"Uppiobummoh!"

"How dare you?" His arm shot out and grabbed her.

"Bleeeerrrcccchhhh! What'd I – e*rrrgghhh* – say?"

"You know what you said, foulfeathers!"

"Uppiobummoh! That's all – *aaaawwwuuulllggghhh* – I said! They're the people who make that seaweed!"

"Uppiobummoh?" He relaxed his grip slightly.

"Uppiobummoh. *Heerrrgghhh!"*

"Hmm. I *do* recall the name on one of those wretched tins, now that you mention it. Arrr." He let go of her and returned his hand to the steering wheel. "And I prefer that you *didn't* mention it again. Anyway, Hieronymous von Nozzel should be able to advise me on our little artefact in the casket. And then ... who knows *what* awaits us?"

"Crark."

"Now, do you have any further questions?"

"Only one." She pecked a few fleas from her tarsus and stared at the roadway ahead. "Are we nearly there yet?"

Jim was standing under the columned parapet of the Temple of Domitian, looking up at one of the remaining statues above him. The stone woman – an ancient goddess, Jim supposed – stared down, her hand on her hip, as if to say, "Hurry! Find him! My world and yours are at risk!"

"Bingo!" screeched Doris.

Jim jumped (he often jumped at her loudness) and

hurried to where she was hopping about on the ground, in front of a marble doorframe set into the hillside.

Brenda and Meltem came too.

"Look!" exclaimed the macaw. "He went in here. See what I found!"

Jim crouched next to her and peered at the object lying in the mud. He got a small twig, speared it through the object, and held it up for all to see.

"What is it?" asked Meltem.

"Quaaaoo," snorted Brenda. She knew what it was.

"You tell her, Doris," said Jim.

Doris blinked, folded her wings behind her tailfeathers, and informed Meltem: "That, Meltem Bottnoff, is evidence that Neptune Flannelbottom Bone was here in this very spot. It is the paper band from one of the world's worst and smelliest cigars: a Belch of Brouhaha Imperial."

Meltem raised a shapely eyebrow.

"The brand preferred by Bone," added Jim. "See the small picture on the band?"

"Ooh. It's the backside of a pig!"

"A Belch of Brouhaha, no question about it."

Brenda, meanwhile, had lumbered to the darkened doorway in the hill. "This looks like some kind of forgotten store-room," she thought.

"Let's look inside that hill," said Jim, putting the cigar band into his pocket with a slight shudder. "It looks like some kind of forgotten store-room. The last few thousand years have put this hill over it all."

Being careful not to slip in the mud, they ventured into the hill. Jim reached into Brenda's saddlebag and took his torch from his knapsack within. He shone the torchlight around the walls.

The Wonder Camel snorted excitedly from a dim corner.

"Rark! Look! Bren's found ... a little bit of candle."

"Good spotting, my lovely." Jim took the candle from her mouth and sniffed the blackened wick. "This was lit in the last few days," he said.

Meltem was inspecting the big mound of mud and earth. "Jim, Doris, Brenda, look here. This slide of mud is recent, too!"

Jim flashed his torchbeam across the mound. Small rivulets of water, seeping through from the hillside, ran down the muddy pile.

"Looks like Bone removed something out of all that." The archaeologist-poet panned his beam across three straight indentations in the mud and dirt. "There was something with straight sides stuck in there." He squatted and had a closer look. "Whatever it was had small egg-shapes on it. See? They've been moulded into the mud."

"Egg-shapes?" cooed Doris. "Maybe it belonged to a bird?"

"Hmm," said Jim.

Then Brenda heard something. She pricked up her ears and listened. "Quaaooo?"

"No, Brenda," said Jim, "I don't think it would've

belonged to a camel. Camels don't lay eggs."

Again she heard the noise, and her Wonder Camel mane bristled. Again she snorted, this time more urgently. "Quaaooo!"

"Not even Wonder Camels," said Jim.

The noise came another time – and now everyone heard it.

A grinding noise.

A dull noise.

A deep, heavy, shifting.

Of rock.

Suddenly the very earth above them groaned – a low, gravelly, unsettling groan, getting louder and louder as it travelled through the hillside.

Then it roared all around them!

"OUT OF HERE!" Jim yelled. "THE HILL'S—"

"Quaaaoooo!"

A huge clod of rock and mud fell, narrowly missing Brenda's fetlock.

"Earthquake!" Meltem shouted.

"VAMOOSE!" screeched Doris, as another rocky clump plunged from the ceiling. She raised her wings and shot towards the door.

Chunks of earth smashed down, exploding like bombs as they hit the ground. The noise tore everything apart, above and to the sides. The ground underfoot and hoof began to fold and buckle, twisting, tearing, grinding, ripping.

"HURRY!" Jim had just pushed Meltem and

Brenda through the doorway, when an enormous slide of mud washed down behind him. *Slooooooooo-oooooooggggghhhhsssssshhhhhhh!*

He tried to dive after his friends, but the onslaught of mud overtook him, rising over the tops of his Sahara boots, swirshling up to his knees. He struggled to move his legs against the deluge, as the avalanching, cracking, *pouring* hillside pushed against his thighs and lower back.

Three seconds later another part of the hillside cracked open, and the sludge burst all around him, shooting up against his chest and neck and bubbling into his mouth. He clamped his lips shut – the wall of mud and earth blinded him – he lost sight of the doorway...

"Jiiiiimmmmm!" He heard Doris's anguished screech before the mud filled his ears.

And then, in a great, rushing burst, the tide of mud lifted him like a beetle in a sea of treacle and carried him out of the door, out of the hillside, out into the daylight, and spat him in a sprawling mess onto the ground.

He picked himself up and ran, following the others, until they were all a safe distance from the store-room. They turned to see the wide stream of mud, grass, dirt and stones oozing out of the doorway.

The domed brickwork above the door cracked apart, and with a mighty roar from the bowels of the earth, the top of the hill collapsed.

SCCCCHHHKKKKKWWWWWWR-
RRRRROOOOOWWWWRRRRRRRHHHH!

In no more than a minute, the store-room of the Temple of Domitian was no more.

And then, more swiftly than it had come, the destruction stopped.

And then there was silence.

Brenda's flanks dripped with sweat, her nostrils flaring in and out.

Doris's chestfeathers rose and fell. "Earthquakes!" she puffed. "I'd rather be moulting than have earthquakes!"

Cairo Jim rubbed his face. Gasping, he looked all around the Temple of Domitian. "Everything out here's fine. The way it was before. The quake only seems to have struck in there."

"Whew!" Meltem wiped the mud from her cheek and sat on one of the foundation slabs of the Temple. "I don't normally get this kind of excitement with my job!"

"Whatever was in there," Jim said, "whatever Bone took from that mud, has survived this. The riddle about that is: will it be a good thing, or a bad thing?"

"A good thing, surely?" puffed Meltem. "Another piece of antiquity has been saved!"

Jim sat next to her and dabbed at a graze on his kneecap. "Sometimes," he said quietly, "I reckon things aren't *meant* to be discovered."

MAN AMONGST THE RUINS

CAIRO JIM WANDERED AROUND the Temple of Domitian, trying to work out what he should do next. Brenda sat with her humps against one of the columns of the parapet, letting the gentle warmth from the marble creep into her spine.

As Jim walked around the ruins, his mind was riddled with questions: where had Bone gone when he had left this place? What had he taken with him from the muddy – now demolished – store-room? What was he up to?

Doris flew over and landed delicately on his shoulder. "So, where do we go from here?" she squawked in his ear.

He was about to open his mouth and tell her he didn't have a clue, when they heard a loud voice coming up the hill.

Meltem stood and raised her hand, signalling to Jim, Doris and Brenda to stay silent. She crouched behind some of the larger foundation stones, and peered over the top.

"May that man have nettle rash in his most unobvious places for the rest of his life!" came the voice. "May he never know what it is to have a good pair

of undergarments! May his whiskers turn inwards and make his eyeballs furry!"

Meltem saw the owner of the voice as he stomped up the hill. She stood and gestured to her friends to follow her.

"Good morning," she called to the old man. He had a white, curly moustache and a bundle of posters under his arm (only the posters were under his arm; the moustache was under his nose). "What's troubling you?"

The old man stopped, stared at her, then at Jim, Doris and Brenda. Then he sat on a marble slab, put down the posters and wiped his neck and forehead with a handkerchief. "What's troubling me? Last night is troubling me, that's what!"

"Last night?" Meltem came and sat by him.

"Would you like some fresh water?" asked Jim, offering his water bottle.

"*Tesukkür ederim*," the man thanked him. He took the bottle and gulped down the cool water. "Mmm. That is the sweetest water that has ever crossed my buds."

Doris winked at Jim – she had filled the water bottle from the Old Relics Society's own 'Spring of Cleopatra – Her Purity is Her Mystery' water cooler before they had left Cairo.

"What happened to you last night?" Meltem asked the old man.

"I should never have been driving at that hour," he frowned, handing the bottle back to Jim. "My daughter, Savine, said to me: 'Father, you are foolish to drive late in the night. There are all kinds of nasty people about on the roads, people you would not want to meet.' But do I listen to Savine?" He shook his head sadly.

"What happened?" Doris asked, hopping onto the marble next to him.

"My car. My little automobile. The cad stole it out from under me!"

Jim crouched in front of the man. "Who? Who stole it?"

"I don't know who it was. I only caught a glimpse of him, and it was dark and my mind was all flustered because Mustafa Kemal Ataturk was all over the road like that." He showed the posters to Meltem. "See? All of these, scattered across the roadway and in the bushes as if they were bits of rubbish!"

Meltem shook her head and made several *tsch-tsch* sounds of deep disapproval.

"I saw these posters of Ataturk, and stopped the car straight away. I was only out of it for a minute, when he slid out from the bushes like a big, dark slug, and oozed his bulk into the front seat of my little car!"

"Did you see what he looked like?" asked Jim. "Anything he was wearing?"

"He was BIG!" answered the old man. "I may have only seen him for a few seconds, but I saw how BIG he was. Fat, fat, fat, fat, like someone had put a bicycle pump into him and inflated him to a point where it is dangerous for a human to be inflated to. He was crammed into that car like a sardine in a can."

"Sounds like Bone," Jim said to Meltem.

"But I *did* see something he was wearing. Something most unusual."

"Yes?" said Jim.

"Yes?" said Meltem.

"Yes?" squawked Doris.

"Quaaooo?"

"A fez!" the old man answered.

Meltem looked at Jim, her dark eyes wide. "That's Bone," she said excitedly. "Only he would wear a fez in Turkey! Mustafa Kemal Ataturk banned the wearing of the fez in this country in 1923."

"And there was the smell," the man went on, his nose crinkling at the memory. "Two smells, actually. The first, like old, rotten prunes. And the second, it was rancid tobacco, the kind that they would never put into Turkish cigarettes."

"Belch of Brouhaha," Doris crowed.

"Was this man carrying anything when he got into the car?" asked Jim urgently.

"Now that you mention it, there *was* something under his arm when he got in. I couldn't make it out clearly in the darkness, but it looked like a sort of box. And it glinted for a moment."

"Like it was made of silver," muttered Cairo Jim.

"Sir, please could you give me your registration details?" Meltem took from her blazer pocket the slimmest mobile phone that Jim, Doris and Brenda had ever seen, and flipped open the cover. "Your number-plate will help us put a trace on the vehicle."

She tapped in a few numbers and then, as the old man told her the information, she relayed it into the phone. When she had finished, she flipped the cover over and slid the phone back into her blazer.

"There. The Antiquities Squad head office is issuing an alert. IMA FATTIE."

Jim looked at her strangely. "Pardon, Meltem?"

"IMA FATTIE."

"Rark!" Doris blinked at her, puzzled. "I don't understand human women. Jocelyn Osgood's just the same. You both have figures that are sensibly curvaceous, and you worry about calories. If you're overweight, Meltem, then I'm a feather duster!"

"IMA FATTIE," Meltem repeated, looking just as puzzled as Doris. "An International Major All-points Felon Alert To Take Immediate Effect."

"Oh," said Jim.

"Rerk."

"Quaaooo."

"Don't worry," Meltem said to the old man, "we'll find your car. And the local branch of the Antiquities Squad will be here soon to take you safely home."

"Tesekkür ederim," he said, gloomily.

"Just one more question," Jim said. "In which direction did he drive off?"

"Hmm. That way. To the north."

All of a sudden 'She'll be Comin' Round the Mountain When She Comes!' started playing from

Meltem's blazer pocket. Meltem looked at Jim, blushed, and then took out her mobile phone. As soon as she flipped open the cover, 'She'll be Comin' Round the Mountain' stopped.

"Senior Retriever of Ancientness Bottnoff speaking." Meltem listened intently. "I see. Mm-hmm. I see. Prunes? I'm not surprised. I see. Good, that gives us something, at least. *Tesekkür ederim,* Romina, and remember: water my saxifraga." She flipped the phone shut and announced, "My colleague, Romina, informs me that the car has been found abandoned in Istanbul. Apparently there's no damage, apart from an offensive odour of prunes and stale cigar smoke, which my colleagues think might need fumigation to clear."

"May the bloated wretch choke on a trumpet," the old man said, but he was happier now he knew about his car.

Jim stood and looked out across the fields and the ruins. "To Istanbul it is, then." He stroked Brenda's snout. "Up to the journey, my lovely? It's a long way."

"Quaaooo." She nodded her head and fluttered her long eyelashes. To be of service to History, and in the company of Cairo Jim and Doris, was her favourite thing in the world. It was even better than reading Western adventure novels.

"You don't mind having an extra human in the saddle?"

Brenda shook her head.

Meltem blushed again. "But, Cairo Jim, do you think it wise for me to be riding so ... so *close* to you?"

Doris rolled her eyes. "Oh, for squawking out loud! It's either there in the saddle, or sitting on the pommel with me!"

Wisely, Meltem decided on the saddle. (It was not a difficult choice to make – the pommel was further from where Jim would be sitting.)

Brenda knelt to the ground. Jim quickly mounted her saddle, made sure Doris was settled on the pommel, helped Meltem on behind him, and then prodded her gently with his boot (Brenda, not Meltem). The Wonder Camel rose and, after they bade farewell to the old man, Brenda began galloping northwards, her hoofs ablaze with urgency.

Desdemona flew through the streets of Istanbul, high over the fez of Neptune Bone. "Crark, have you got ants in your pants or something? You're almost *skipping* down there!"

He blew an acrid column of smoke in her general direction, and continued along, past the majestic but neglected Aya Sofya (once one of the most splendid domed churches in all the world), and through the gathering hordes of tourists that were stumbling out of the big buses that had brought them there. "My gait is full of anticipation," he said to the raven.

"Eh? What gate? We never came through any—"

"My *walk*, you moronic mess of manginess. I am fairly itching with eagerness."

"You should wash your underwear more often," she croaked.

"Cease your disgusting drivel! Come, this way. There is a sokak* up here that will take us to the Istanbul Archaeological Museum, away from these ignorant and noisy crowds."

"Oh, for badness' sakes, not another museum! Sheesh, we've been in more museums than we've had hot baths! Why d'we have to go to another museum? They give me the willies – all those staring white statues and strange marble creatures. Yeeerggghh!"

"Because, since he retired from the world, Professor von Nozzel has lived in his small apartment within the Istanbul Archaeological Museum's walls. That is where we are to find him."

He continued bounding along, and Desdemona kept flying with him, past the Blue Mosque, through the ancient Hippodrome which had been the hub of life in this city for 1400 years, past the Egyptian Obelisk of Theodosius (Bone had paused momentarily before it to announce in a tone full of admiration that it had been 'a mighty plunderous effort to get that thing here') until they came to the top of a hill, and a smaller, cobbled road.

Down this road there was a large gate on the right.

---

* Street

Bone stopped, and the raven descended and perched on his flabby shoulder.

"Here is the Archaeological Museum," he told her. "And if what's in this casket is what I think it is, then it will put all the treasures within this museum to pale and watery insignificance! Arrrrrrr."

OLD EXISTENCE

WHILE BONE WALKED through the halls and corridors lined with white and yellowing marble busts and statues, his Crimplene plus-fours trousers swished and his thighs trembled with anticipation.

Desdemona hop-flutter-skidded on the slippery granite tiles. "Crark! It's so cold in here! Clammy. You mean ta say this von Nozzel guy lives in here with these statues. Yergh, that's creepy!"

"Shhh, keep your croaking down. The less people know we're here, the better for us."

He stopped behind a foreboding-looking statue of Agrippina the Elder, and peered around the statue's shoulder. Desdemona slid to a halt, her talons squealing on the floor until she banged into the back of Bone's leg.

"Arrr, watch it, you slippery simpleton!" He tightened his arm around the silver casket.

"Erk," she erked, having got a beakful of his prune-whiffy back regions.

"There it is," he whispered, spying a small sign above a door at the end of the hallway.

NO ADMITTANCE. MUSEUM STAFF ONLY
AND PROF. H. VON NOZZEL.
TRESPASSERS WILL BE PERSECUTED.

"That's where he hangs out," said Bone, more to himself than to the raven. He ashed his cigar on the top of Agrippina the Elder's head – the ash did not look at all obvious amongst the carved curls there – and looked around. "Come, Desdemona, and don't muck about on the tiles any more."

"Sheesh," she said, following him to the door.

His pudgy hand grabbed the doorknob and tried to twist it. "Confound it. Locked."

"So? Stick your arm out."

The raven hop-fluttered onto his arm and lowered her head so her beak was level with the keyhole. She inserted the very tip of her beak into the hole and wriggled her jaws, making a strange noise with her vocal chords as she did so. (To Bone, it sounded as if she were saying, 'The bus belongs to Desmond Tutu' with a beakful of marbles.)

There was a sharp *click*, and she withdrew her beaktip. "There," she said, her eyes throbbing redly. "Try the doorknob now."

Bone did so. This time it turned, and the door opened silently.

"For once, you did something right," he sneered at her. "Quickly, follow me."

"What a mountain of gratitude," she croaked, hopping after him into the dim, wide corridor.

They crept past many boxes and crates, some opened and others sealed. All of them were caked in dust. In the opened crates lay many old, broken pots and vases and small, unremarkable, ancient bronze figurines.

The only light that penetrated the corridor came from a small, grimy skylight set high above.

"Doesn't look like anyone's been through here for centuries," sniffed Desdemona.

"Quiet!"

Bone approached a large sarcophagus that was nearly as deep as he was tall, and which took up most of the end section of the corridor. The carvings on the sarcophagus were smothered in so much dust, it was hard to tell whether the small carved figures were men, women, gods or beasts. They looked like dust blobs with legs and arms; strange creatures from the Land of Neglect.

Bone stopped by the sarcophagus and peered hard at the wall to the right of it. As his eyes adjusted to this gloomier part of the corridor, he began to see an outline: the outline of a doorframe, carved in the Oriental style with a pointed top and rounded sides. The door set into this frame was made of old, dusty, latticed wood, which had blackened with age.

On the lattice in the centre of the door was a small brass plaque, engraved in Turkish and English with the words:

PROFESSOR HIERONYMOUS VON NOZZEL.

B.ARCH., M.ANTQ., PH.D., ETC., ETC., ETC.

(RETIRED)

Bone looked at Desdemona, and she at him. Then he pounded his flabby fist against the lattice door,

and a decade's-worth of dust exploded silently from the woodwork.

The air was filled with the thick bombardment. It made Bone's nostrils twitch violently, and Desdemona's fleas bite harder than ever. Man and raven had to hold their breath, lest they should sneeze so ferociously that something inside them might pop out or become dislodged.

And then, as the dust started to settle heavily like a snowfall, an old, wavering voice called from behind the lattice: "Y-y-yes? Is someone there?"

"Is someone there," muttered Bone, rolling his eyes.

"Maybe the termites round here are mighty aggressive," suggested Desdemona.

"Come in, if y-y-you are there," the voice called again.

With an arrogant sweep of his arm, Bone thrust open the lattice door. He held the silver casket close to his chest, and entered a tall room, the floorspace of which was barely bigger than the inside of a double wardrobe. The raven slunk in after him.

One wall of this minuscule room was taken up with a narrow, floor-to-ceiling bookshelf, filled with hundreds of old, falling-apart volumes. The only other furniture in the room was a small, narrow bed, a thin, narrow table piled high with papers and books and Barry Manilow records, and a rickety, insubstantial chair.

In this chair sat a man with cobweb-hair and skin like parchment. He wore small spectacles with glass in them so thick that it looked as if his eyes were swimming in some clear liquid on the other side of the frames. He was dressed in a threadbare dressing-gown which he wore across a light-grey pinstriped suit.

As Bone tried to find a place to stand, the old man blinked curiously at him.

"Professor von Nozzel," Bone smiled, the cigar between his lips sticking straight up.

"I remember y-y-you," said Hieronymous von Nozzel. "It's y-y-young Neptune Bone."

"Arrr," nodded the fleshy man.

"Oh, y-y-yes, I remember y-y-you all right. You used to skip most of my lectures... What were y-y-you doing? Ah, that's right – you were up at the pyramids all the time, trying to sell those ghastly plastic ushabtis and scarabs to the tourists. You used to claim they w-w-were ancient and genuine!"

"A youthful lark," giggled Bone. "Professor, I have come to see you to—"

"And then, when it was examination time, y-y-you tried to bribe me – with a box of some hideous chocolates – to give you the exam papers before the day. You were a scoundrel then, you were. I hope y-y-you've changed your ways since!"

"Many of the things I did when I was younger are a great embarrassment to me now, Professor von Nozzel. I have changed completely."

"You've got fatter, that's for sure." The old man peered at Bone's bulging emerald-green waistcoat.

"If I'd known y-y-you were coming, I'd have got the builders in."

Desdemona sniggered in the corner.

"Professor, let us put the past behind us."

"There's no room to put *anything* behind you," croaked the raven, eyeing Bone's enormous backside pressed against the bookshelf.

"What do you w-w-want?" asked Professor von Nozzel suspiciously.

"I have come," Bone informed him in a voice rippling with the prospect of unbridled excitement, "to show you something I have found. I have an idea what it is, but I need you – with your comprehensive and encyclopaedic knowledge of ancient gods and cults – to verify my discovery."

The Professor looked up at him through his thick spectacles. He licked his cracked, dry lips. "What have you got, then?"

Bone swept the pile of papers, books and Barry Manilow records off the table and onto the floor. A mushroom-cloud of dust erupted, but he paid it no heed. "Behold," he announced, gently laying the silver casket on the table.

Professor von Nozzel leaned forward at once. His eyes widened. "A nice piece," he said. "Very fine condition. It is rare to find such a piece nowadays, especially with all the egg motifs intact as these are. I'd date it to pre-Hellenistic. It is astonishing that the silver has survived in such fine condition."

"Arrr." Bone puffed on his cigar.

Desdemona watched through slitted, throbbing eyes.

"But," continued the Professor, "the casket itself is relatively unremarkable. It w-w-would not be out of place in a museum such as this one, but it would be overshadowed by many other finer and greater relics."

"It's not the casket I brought to show you," Bone purred, "but what's inside it!"

He sprung open the lid and delved inside the casket. Delicately, as though he was holding a huge piece of the finest gossamer woven from a butterfly's breath, he unravelled a long, white length of fabric. A garment from ancient times.

Hieronymous von Nozzel felt his pulse quicken. He watched as Bone held the garment against himself, displaying it as if he were a model on a catwalk.

"Is this not a find of great magnitude, Professor?"

Von Nozzel let his gaze wander slowly over the garment, so that he could take in the sight of all the intricate needlework: the many exquisitely placed tucks; the beautiful pattern of bulbous shapes sown on the front; the heavy, draping folds and the tiny design of egg-shaped pleatings and embroidery that decorated the hemline and sleeve borders.

As Bone held it in the dusty light, it seemed to radiate a glow – a soft, pure, white glow that bathed everything around it in its wash.

Hieronymous von Nozzel's heart was pumping faster now. Tiny beads of moisture were appearing on his forehead, and dotting his palms. "Could it be?" he stammered, his jaw trembling.

"You tell me," said Neptune F. Bone.

"Oh, such beauty!" The Professor took a pair of white gloves from the pocket of his dressing-gown, and slipped them onto his hands. He ran his gloves gently across the garment, across the bulbous shapes drooping on the front.

"Arrr," Bone squirmed.

"It is beauty of the finest order," whispered von Nozzel. "Never w-w-would I have thought that this could be as stunning as it is. The legends and the histories never recorded its exact appearance, only the w-w-way She wore it."

"And so is it what I think it is?" Bone hissed, hardly able to contain his curiosity.

"You have found that which has eluded scholars, archaeologists and hunters of history for thousands of y-y-years. Yes, Bone, you have stumbled upon the very garment w-w-worn by the greatest goddess from Greek and Roman antiquity, She who was the twin sister of Apollo Himself!"

"Tell me, tell me! Let me hear it from your learned lips, Professor von Nozzel! *What is this garment?*"

"You have found the long-lost Petticoat of the Great Goddess Artemis!"

"Bog me down and dredge me!" croaked Desdemona.

"I knew it," Bone said, his eyes brimming with great

glee. "I knew this wasn't just some old bit of ancient froufrou. Your recognition of it confirms what I suspected."

"Oh," the Professor gasped, "what a find! What a magnificent stroke of luck that you—" He suddenly stopped, and peered into the casket. "Tell me, was there anything else in here? A gold-and-silver belt, perhaps?"

"No." Bone shook his head. "Just this. Why?"

"Perhaps that is a good thing," von Nozzel said quietly. "According to my research, this Petticoat of Artemis imbued the goddess with enormous power, provided She w-w-wore it with the Belt of Bountaiety. In fact, from what I uncovered when I wrote my book *At the End of the Deities*, it seemed that any w-w-woman – not just the goddess Artemis – could have the power of the Petticoat, provided she was w-w-wearing the Belt of Bountaiety with it."

"Is that so?" asked Bone.

"Y-y-yes. There's a copy of *At the End of the Deities* on the shelf up there ... see, that big, red-leather bound volume, between the Atlas and Charmaine Solomon's *Complete Asian Cookbook*."

"And one would have to possess this Belt of Bountaiety in order for the power of the Petticoat of Artemis to work?" Bone asked the question slowly, his eyes needling into the old man.

"According to what I have gathered from ancient legends and histories. It is a fascinating story, Bone; y-y-you should read it after you donate the Petticoat to the museum here. It might even round off the education y-y-you kept dodging, w-w-way back at Archaeology School."

"Crark," gloated Desdemona. "That's telling you, you tubby truant!"

"Arrr, I'll read it, all right," growled the fleshy man, as he quickly rolled up the Petticoat and put it back into the casket. Then he pulled out his fob-watch and unhooked its rose-gold chain from his waistcoat buttonhole. "I've been reading another book lately, a small tome entitled *Have Your Way with the World: A Beginner's Guide to the Joys of Hypnotism*. And look what I have learned!"

He held the chain between himself and the Professor, and slowly, silently, the gold fob-watch began to swing. Back and forth, back and forth, the gold glinting at the crest of each arc of the swinging.

Hieronymous von Nozzel's eyeballs locked onto the watch, and followed its movement back and forth, back and forth, back and ever-forth...

...while Neptune Bone whispered a directive of dreadful deviousness.

8

GRAPPLING WITH REALITY

AS BRENDA THE WONDER CAMEL approached the sprawling outskirts of the largest city in Turkey, Cairo Jim's poetry cells – spurred on by Brenda's galloping and her steady, repetitive movement – intermingled with her rhythm. A verse sprang up, and Jim didn't realise he was speaking it aloud:

> "He's raiding History once again,
> > this brute the size of eighteen men,
> this cad, this bad and bloated fool,
> > so here we are at Istanbul."

"Erk!" Doris winced her beak. She had the highest opinion of Jim's talents as an *archaeologist*.

Meltem listened to his poetic murmuring, and a gentle tingling crept through her arms as she held tightly onto his waist.

"Quaaooo!" Brenda snorted the dust from the last couple of hundred kilometres out of her strong but sensitive nostrils.

Then there was another loud burst of 'She'll be Comin' Round the Mountain When She Comes!', so sudden that Doris jumped on the pommel, and

Brenda almost lost her pace.

"You're popular, Meltem," called Cairo Jim over his shoulder.

"You can call me Mel, if you'd prefer," she said, removing her right arm from around his waist and taking her phone from inside her blazer. She flipped open the cover and spoke in her serious manner. "Senior Retriever of Ancientness Bottnoff speaking. *Merhaba*, Romina. On a Wonder Camel. No, neither did I." She paused and her finely shaped eyebrows rose with interest. "Really? When was this? I see. Do we know where ... ah. Well, at least that's something to go on. Cairo Jim, Doris, Brenda and I will go straight there." She listened some more, and raised her eyebrows. "Please try to save it. *Teşekkür ederim*, Romina." She snapped the cover shut and put the phone away.

"News?" Jim called.

"Yes. My *Bergenia cordifolia* has fungus."

"Erk," squawked Doris.

"Saxifraga," explained Meltem.

Jim squirmed. "No, about Bone?"

"Oh, yes." She pushed the thought of her pot plant to the back of her mind. "The IMA FATTIE has been effective. Bone was seen leaving the Archaeological Museum yesterday morning. He had his raven with him, and was carrying what looked like a box."

"Do we know where he went?" asked Doris.

Meltem shook her head. "Our scout followed him,

but unfortunately lost sight of him in the crowds. Bone seemed headed towards Taksim Square."

Jim thought hard as Brenda whizzed through the ever-increasing traffic. The Archaeological Museum? Was there any possible reason for Bone going there, apart from plunder? Was there any link between—

The image of his old Professor from Archaeology School entered his mind, like a pale figure hurtling urgently through a cobwebbed doorway. "Of course!" blurted the archaeologist-poet. "I remember now! He retired there!"

"Quaaooo," snorted Brenda, as the image came into her mind as well, even though she had never met Hieronymous von Nozzel.

"Who?" Doris flexed herself up and down on the pommel. "Who, who, who?"

"You'll see, my dear." He gently prodded Brenda with his Sahara boot. "My lovely," he shouted, "turn right at the next sokak!"

"Whoa, Brenda!" commanded Jim, forty minutes later. She halted before the steps of the enormous Istanbul Archaeological Museum, in the expansive courtyard filled with small monuments, weathered stone sarcophaguses, faded ancient gravestones and other historical pieces that for various reasons were not considered important enough to be housed within the museum's walls.

"Down, my lovely."

A gentle prod of Jim's boot brought Brenda slowly

to the ground. Cairo Jim leapt off and extended his hand to assist Meltem.

Doris blinked at all the windows. "Rark. Never have I seen so many windows in a museum. There're more panes of glass up there than I could poke my beak at, if I were a parrot with nothing better to do with my time."

"It's vast, isn't it?" Meltem stepped from the saddle, her hand almost disappearing in Jim's. For an instant she left it there, feeling the warmth of his palm. Then, simultaneously, they let go, and Jim got Brenda's water dish quickly out of the saddle bag.

Meltem turned to face the museum again. "Let me tell you something about this place, Doris. You see all those windows?"

"Prerk."

"Many years ago, the museum staff counted all those windows from the outside. There are just as many on the other side of the museum, and many more at both ends as well. A huge number, in total. Then the museum staff went inside, and counted the windows again. All over the building. Do you know what they discovered?"

"What?" Doris's crest arched forward with curiosity.

"They found that when they counted the windows from the *inside*, they couldn't find fifty-three of the windows. Every time they did the counting, there were fifty-three windows *missing*."

The macaw blinked, and a strange chill rushed through her feathers.

"The place is so very big," continued Meltem, "that there are places within it that are unaccounted for."

"Like History itself," said Jim, watching Brenda slurp the water he had poured into the bowl. "The whole of History is so sweeping, there are pockets back there that everyone's forgotten about. But they're still around, as we've found many times. Isn't that right, Doris?"

"Too right," she squawked. Then something in the courtyard garden caught her eye, and she let out an electrifying screech. *"SSSCCCCCCCCCCRRRRAAAA-AAAAAAAAAAAAAARKKKKKKK!"*

"Quaaaoooooooooooooo!" Brenda jumped at the racket.

"Wh-what is it?" asked Jim, his heart beating faster.

"O-o-over there," Doris stammered, flexing her wings and jumping onto Jim's shoulder. "All around those statues and gravestones!"

Dozens of furry shadows slunk in and out of the stonework.

"Cats!" said Meltem.

"Eecrk," wailed Doris.

Jim reached up and patted her crestfeathers. "Don't worry, my dear, they won't get near you. I'll make sure of that."

She folded her wing around his neck, and shuddered.

Brenda rolled her head in a wide circle. *"So will I,"* she thought strongly.

"Let's go in and find Professor von Nozzel," Jim said. "We need him to shed some light, and quickly."

After walking and fluttering through the echoing halls and galleries filled with sculptures so beautiful that Jim had to work hard to keep his goosebumps under control (lest he should end up looking like a human-sized version of one of those small rubber things with knobbly bits all over it that people put on their thumbs when they have to count sheets of paper), they came to the doorway that led to von Nozzel's passage.

Doris read aloud the plaque on the door. "Rark, looks like we go through there. I guess it's okay, even if we're not museum staff."

"Don't get your feathers in a fluster about that," said Meltem. "The Antiquities Squad has priority in any museum in the world."

Jim turned the doorknob. "Unlocked," he said, pushing the door slowly open.

"Quickly," Meltem urged, entering the dim, wide corridor. Jim and Doris followed, and Brenda brought up the rear.

"You know," Jim said softly as they passed the dusty boxes and crates lining the walls, "way back at Archaeology School, Professor von Nozzel was one of the most popular teachers we had. He was so brilliant – I was sure there wasn't a single thing he didn't know about the ancient gods and religions. But he wasn't stingy or mean with all that knowledge. No, he was always more than willing to share what he knew with his students, all of whom who were eager to get out into the field and uncover more of what he was teaching."

Brenda's hoofs clacked loudly along on the granite floor.

"Then," said Jim, "he retired, and came here to write his life's work: *At the End of the Deities*. As a matter of fact, the archaeological world has all but forgotten about him. Sad how that happens so often."

Meltem stopped by the large sarcophagus at the end of the corridor. "There's a doorway in the gloom," she whispered. "See the lattice?"

Before Jim knew it, he was blurting directly from his poetry cells:

"There's a doorway in the gloom
that'll lead us to a room
where History is thriving fit to burst;
where a man might hold the key
for all of archaeology,
that'll stop that cad from carrying out the—"

"Jim!" Doris snapped tersely. "This is no time for poetry!"

Cairo Jim blushed, but Brenda snorted admiringly.

"Look," observed Meltem. "There's a plaque."

Four sets of eyes adjusted to the dimness. In silence, they read the inscription on the door's plaque.

"This is it," Jim said quietly. He raised his fist and knocked politely but firmly on the door.

In a blink of a second, the air was filled with dust – ancient, sweetish-smelling, thick, powdery dust, which blasted out of the lattice and into their faces, beak and snout.

Unfortunately, Brenda's nostrils were wide open, and the barrage of tiny particles shot straight into her nose. She jerked her head back, clamping her nostrils shut with her unique nostril-clenching muscles, but it was too late – with a great gulping in of the dusty air, Brenda sneezed a colossal sneeze.

"AH-AH-AH-QUUUUU-AAA-AAA-AAA-AAA-AA-AAA-OOOOOOOOO!"

The blast from her snout smacked hard against the wooden door and blew it wide open with a loud crash. Another cloud of dust billowed around it.

And then there was silence as the particles began to settle.

Brenda held her breath tightly so she wouldn't sneeze again.

Doris quivered the dust from her feathers.

Meltem looked at Jim and noticed that his sun-spectacles were wonky.

Jim looked at Meltem and noticed that she was looking at him.

Doris looked at Jim looking at Meltem looking at Jim.

Brenda looked at Doris looking at Jim and being looked at by Meltem.

Jim looked at Brenda looking at Doris.

This would have gone on for a lot longer, had it not been for a strange noise that burst forth from Professor von Nozzel's room.

"KA-KA-KA-KA-KA-KA-KA-KA-KA-KAHA-HA-HA-HAHAHAHAHAHAHAHA-KA-KA-KA-KA!"

"What in the name of Boadicea was that?" squawked Doris, raising her wings in alarm.

"Let's find out," said Jim. Tentatively he entered the small room, followed by Meltem. Brenda sensed the room's tiny proportions and sensibly decided to remain in the corridor.

Jim, Doris and Brenda saw the towering, crammed bookshelf, the narrow bed and the table, the floor littered with papers and books and Barry Manilow records, and the rickety chair in the room's centre.

But Professor von Nozzel was not sitting in the chair. Instead, with both his hands tucked firmly under the armpits of his threadbare dressing-gown, he was perched on the top of the chair's back and, with an alarming expulsion of noise, he emitted once again the sharp, loud, laughing call of the common Australian kookaburra.

BIRD ABSURD

"KA-KA-KA-KA-KA-KA-KA-KA-KA-KA-HAHAHA-HAHAHAHAHAHA-KA-KA-KA-KA!"

The laughing cry shot out of Hieronymous von Nozzel's gullet with all the ferocity of demented machine-gun fire.

Jim stepped back against the bookshelf behind him. Doris quickly hopped off his shoulder and up onto the only empty space on the shelves, while Meltem frowned uncertainly.

Then Jim extended his hand. "Professor von Nozzel? It's me, Jim of Cairo. One of your students from years ago."

The old, cobwebby man threw back his head and, shutting one eye and fixing the other firmly on his visitors, he let forth another volley: *"KA-KA-KA-KA-KA-KA-KA-KA-KA-KAHAHAHA-HAHAHAHAHAHAHAHA-KA-KA-KA-KA!"*

Outside in the corridor, Brenda's nostrils flared at the racket.

"Rark," rarked Doris when the commotion had died down. "That's one welcome we've never yet had."

Cairo Jim jiggled a finger about in his left ear, and

Meltem massaged the sides of her face, close to her cheekbones.

The Professor continued to sit there, eyeing them shrewdly. Occasionally he raised his elbows a fraction, as though he was considering flying up to the high ceiling.

Jim tried again. "Professor, do you remember me?"

"*Ka-ka-ka-ka!*"

"Do you remember *you*?"

The only response to that was a twitch of Hieronymous von Nozzel's rear portions on top of the chair. Still the beady stare continued.

"What on earth's wrong with him?" asked Meltem.

"Maybe it's all this isolation," Jim said. "It might have taken its toll."

"*I'll* tell you what's wrong with him," Doris said in her authority voice. "He thinks he's a bird, that's what it is."

"A bird?" repeated Jim.

"A bird?" Meltem said.

"Quaoo quaooo?" came a snort from the corridor.

"Yes," blinked the macaw, "and not just any old bird. No, I recognise that call. It belongs to the kookaburra, a large arboreal kingfisher native to Australia. I actually met one once, when we were in Burkina-Faso of all places. He was called Brian, and he'd accidentally got caught in a wonky wind current that'd carried him all the way from Dubbo."

"Dubbo?" said Meltem.

"Apparently such a place exists." Doris was flexing herself up and down on the bookshelf. "He was a real laughing jackass, I'm telling you!"

"A kookaburra?" Jim gasped. "But why? How did the Professor come to this?"

Meltem sighed sadly. "I wonder how long he's been this way?"

The Professor cocked his head and watched Doris on the shelf above. She was still flexing up and down, and Professor von Nozzel started doing the same, in rhythm, with his neck and head.

"*Too* long," answered Jim of Cairo, a feeling of dread spreading slowly through his stomach and legs.

"Arrrr, listen to this, grotbucket."

In a gloomy corner booth in the once grand but now faded bar of the Hotel Pera Palas, the hotel built in 1868 for the travellers on the Orient Express, Neptune Bone was excitedly perusing the pages of von Nozzel's *At the End of the Deities*, which he had stolen from the Professor's bookshelves after he had hypnotised him.

"What?" croaked Desdemona, her eyes throbbing redly.

"This bit from the chapter entitled 'The Demise of Artemis'. This is what will help me wreak my Genius across the entire world!"

"Go on, go on, you have my full and underided attention." She pecked at a working party of fleas who were holding a debate in her nether feathers.

Bone exhaled a shaft of Belch of Brouhaha smoke and cleared his throat: "Aherm.

"'Part Three – The Legendary Petticoat of Artemis. After public opinion had been turned against the Great Goddess Artemis, almost anything to do with Her – any statuary or religious relic – was destroyed. But one major item escaped destruction: the bountiful Petticoat worn by Artemis Herself!

"'How this came to survive, and then be lost again, can be read about in a further chapter. The Power of the Petticoat is what concerns us here. According to accounts of the time, she who wore the Petticoat of Artemis, around which was buckled the gold-and-silver Belt of Bountaiety, would have untold powers of fruitfulness.'"

Bone paused and looked up, his eyes glinting with a primeval greed.

"What's so good about that?" Desdemona rasped. "Too much fruit's a bad thing. If you eat too many plums, for instance, you get the—"

"Clamp shut your beak, you cretinous conglomeration of confusion. Listen to what von Nozzel says:

"'These powers would allow the wearer of the Petticoat to bring forth blossoms and fruit on hitherto dead trees and plants; to make water run again along dry and barren riverbeds; to turn scorched tracts of dirt into rich and fertile soil; to create greenery where there had been dust, and to generally make all things fruitful, prosperous and life-giving.'"

"Well tie me to a trellis and call me Wisteria!"

"Arrr." Bone slapped the book shut. "I've no time to waste, if this plan that I'm devising is to take root." A sudden idea lunged into his fat head. He snapped his chubby fingers urgently in the air. "Waiter!"

A man in a black bow-tie came rushing to the booth.

"Bring me a telephone," Bone commanded. "I need to make an urgent long-distance call."

"Yes, sir," said the waiter. "But first I must ask you: are you staying at our hotel?"

"Why of course I am," he lied with a flabby smile. "I am ensconced in your Mrs Wallis Simpson suite."

"Very good, sir." He bowed and quickly brought the phone to Bone's table.

"Thank you, now go away. I need privacy."

The waiter bowed and left.

Desdemona watched as Bone dialled a number. "Who're you calling?" she asked, hopping up onto the table and peering into the phone.

"An associate I once knew from my younger days. He lives in a small country from which I was harshly and forcibly deported."

"Crark."

The phone line crackled and rang for a long time. Then there was a click, and a faint voice answered.

"Hello? Bellonius Wasteland Real Estate. Dirt Cheap Land Across the Globe. Slobodan Bellonius speaking."

"Slobby, you wretch. Neptune Bone here."

"Bone? Neptune Bone? I thought you were dead."

"No doubt a case of mistaken identity. Now look, I need to buy all that worthless land you have. You know the area – all of that useless wilderness east of Ankara, right across to the borders of Georgia, Armenia and Iran."

"You want that? But the soil's hopeless! You couldn't get your toenails to grow in it, and no one would ever want to live out there. It's worse than Siberia! And what about all those mountains?"

"Slobby, I want that land!" Bone's beard was bristling.

"Well, if you're really set on it, I'll let you have it dirt cheap. Ha ha ha! Get it? *Dirt cheap*, as in—"

"You'll let me have it for *nothing*, you deceitful man."

"Ha ha ha. For nothing? You should get a bigger hat, Bone. Those fezzes don't protect your head enough from the sun. Why should I give you all that land for nothing? It's more than 150,000 square kilometres!"

"Because of a certain photograph I have of you."

Slobodan Bellonius fell silent. The line crackled and hissed.

Bone said, "Did you hear me, Slobby?"

"You've got nothing on me, Bone. That could be anybody in that wax museum."

"Arrr, I think not. I don't imagine there are too many men with a large birthmark resembling the *Titanic*, right in the middle of their—"

"All right," snapped the voice of Bellonius. "That's enough about that!"

"And the photo of you that I captured for all of eternity, involved as you were in that wax museum with Catherine the Great, Genghis Khan and Bing Crosby, would create more than a few ripples throughout the Real Estate profession. Why, heavens to the Goddess Betsy, you could be struck off the register. Not to mention the foreign implications involving Russia, China and the United States of America. Your tiny country could be plunged into war with them all if I were to make this photo public..."

"Yes, yes, yes, you've made your point. Okay, you get the land. Where do you want me to send the deeds?"

"To Mr Impluvium, care of the Hotel Pera Palas, Istanbul. I shall alert the people on the front desk to expect the package."

"Mr Impluvium?"

"An alias. I'm sure you understand about aliases, don't you, Slobby?"

"The deeds will be there the day after tomorrow. You are slimeball of the universe, Bone."

"And I dream about you every night, too, Slobby. Thank you so much for your co-operation."

Several very rude words came down the line, and then Bone blew two loud and wet kisses, slammed the receiver down and smiled. "I knew he'd see things my way. Now it's just a matter of time, and power will start dribbling back into my hands. Think of it, Desdemona, 150,000 square kilometres of land, all of it mine, all of it worthless *now*, but soon, after I have worked the magic of the Petticoat of Artemis upon it, all of it will be so valuable, so rich and desirable, so very much a paradise, the likes of which—"

"There's just one thing, my Captain. One tiny thing that might put a little spanner in your underpants."

"And what might that be, you odious ornithological oddball?"

"We still have to get hold of this Belt of Bountaiety, don't we? Didn't the book say that you had to have that as well as the Petticoat?"

Bone ashed his cigar onto her head. "Arrr. For once, you're right." He quickly opened *At the End of the Deities* to its index of gods, and ran his plump index finger down the entries under B: "Let's see... Baal, Bachamus, Balder, Bapedis, Barangas, Barry Manilow... Ah! Here it is – *Belt of Bountaiety*, page 692."

His fat hands flipped the pages back until he came to the desired location. His pudgy eyeballs sleered down the page, then stopped. Like two plump caterpillars getting excited, his eyebrows bristled and crept up his broad forehead.

"What?" croaked Desdemona, when his eyebrows could go no further. "Whaddasit say?"

Bone slapped the volume shut and puffed earnestly on his cigar. "We have another little journey ahead of us," he rumbled quietly.

"Crark. What about von Nozzel? Is it safe to leave him back there at that museum?"

"Have no concern for him. He is absolutely

immersed in his state of kookaburradness. The only thing that'll get him out of that is a swinging object and the words 'Throw back your beak and crow.' No, he'll be quite out of the way and harmless. We shall stay here at the Pera Palas Hotel until Slobby's deeds arrive. That'll give me two days to have my fingernails pampered in the Coco Chanel Manicure Salon upstairs, before we embark upon our journey."

"Where? Where we journeyin' to this time?"

"To the ancient ruins of Aphrodisias," he answered, as a look of gross thoughtfulness crept into his eyes, and he cracked his knuckles loudly.

THE REDISCOVERY OF VON NOZZEL

"'WILL YE NOT OBSERVE the strangeness of his alter'd countenance?'" Doris quoted from *Henry VI, Part II* by William Shakespeare. She was now hanging upside down from the bookshelf above Hieronymous von Nozzel's head, and swinging in a state of high agitation.

Jim, Meltem and Brenda stared at the preening Professor. As Doris moved backwards and forwards, she kept her eyes on the Professor's. He followed her, his head cocking to the left and then to the right, in time to her swinging.

"He really is gone," Doris said sadly.

Von Nozzel twitched his arm-wings and gave a small cry: *"Ka-ka-ka-ka!"*

Cairo Jim took off his pith helmet. He didn't know what to do. Half of him was feeling despair for his old Professor, and the other half – the half that made Jim's stomach watery and uneasy – was filling with foreboding about what Neptune Bone was plotting.

Doris continued swinging upside down from the shelf. "Rark! Snap out of it, Professor!" she squawked loudly.

His head moved back and forth, in time to her swinging. *"Ka-ka-ka-ka!"*

"Oh, for crowing out loud!" said the macaw. "That's no way to be a bird! If you want to be one of us, at least be *proud* of yourself. We birds are a noble race, after all!"

"Ka-ka-ka!"

The more flustered Doris was getting, the quicker she was swinging. "Come on, man! Puff out your chest-feathers! Let the world know who you are! Being a bird – any kind of bird – is a great honour! Proclaim it to the furthest treetop! Go on, tell everybody! None of this tininess, this ka-ka-ka timidity!"

"Pra-ka-ka-ka—"

"That's it! THROW BACK YOUR BEAK AND CROW!"

With a sudden jerk, Professor von Nozzel pulled his hands out from under his armpits, pointed a frail forefinger at Jim, and spoke furiously. "It might even round off the education y-y-you kept dodging, w-w-way back at Archaeology School, y-y-you overblown great—"

"Rark," rarked Doris. She stopped swinging and hung still.

"Professor?" said Jim.

The Professor blinked his eyes and peered at him. "W-w-wait a moment! You're not Neptune Bone!"

"No, Professor, it's me, Jim of Cairo."

Von Nozzel looked down and saw that he was balanced on the top of the back of his chair. "What in the name of Pegasus? Whoooaaahhhh!" He twitched, lost his balance, and slid forward, down onto the seat. "Oof."

"You thought you were a kookaburra," Jim told him.

"A kookaburra?" The old man blinked, his oversized eyes opening and closing like two great doorways behind his thick spectacles. He scratched his wispy hair. "That cad," he muttered. "That evil w-w-windbag, he must have hypnotised me! Y-y-yes, the fob watch, the fob watch..."

Jim introduced Doris, Brenda and Meltem Bottnoff. Then he asked the Professor about Bone.

"Oh, I remember every detail of his visit, Jim. It's as if it all happened only three seconds ago."

With almost breathless urgency, von Nozzel told them of his encounter with Bone and the raven. As Jim listened, his eyebrows prickled with dread.

"The long-lost Petticoat of Artemis?" Jim's voice was almost smothered by flabbergastedness. "But it's been missing for millennia! Bone's got it?"

"That he has," nodded von Nozzel. "The blackguard. Brought it here in a beautiful silver casket decorated with Artemis' gold fertility symbols. Small egg shapes, in a border all around the lid. The Petticoat is magnificent, believe me! I swear it *glowed* when Bone held it up!"

Meltem whipped out her notebook and started writing.

"And," von Nozzel continued, "by the looks of that gap where Doris is swinging on the bookshelves there – incidentally, *tesekkür ederim*, Doris, for saving me from my bird-like state... I was starting to get a craving for a lizard or two – y-y-you came through just in time—"

"You're very welcome," said Doris.

"What about that gap, Professor?"

"Mm? Oh, the gap, y-y-yes. I'd say Bone's taken my only copy of *At the End of the Deities*. So he's got that, too, which means..." His voice trailed off, and a great frown made the wrinkles on his face multiply by dozens.

"Which means what?" A trickle of perspiration ran down Jim's forehead, and Meltem looked up anxiously from her notebook.

"Which means he knows where to look for the Belt."

"Quaaooo?" Brenda snorted from the hallway.

"I remember now," Jim said, as tiny details of Professor von Nozzel's lectures started creeping back into his mind. "The Belt of Bountaiety!"

"That indeed," said von Nozzel grimly.

Meltem shut her notebook. "Please, Professor, I am not understanding. What exactly *is* this Petticoat of Artemis? What does it represent? What can Bone possibly do with it, apart from sell it on the antiquities black market? And what does this Belt of ... of Bountaiety have to do with things?"

The old man gripped the sides of his chair and, with a tiny grunt, lifted himself to his feet. "Come, let me show you something here in the museum. Something that might make everything a bit clearer, for there is a story involved in all of this that reaches far back into History."

Twenty minutes later, the Professor led them all into a small gallery in the northern wing of the Istanbul Archaeological Museum. He fumbled about with his hand on the wall until he found the light switch. There was a loud *click* and the gallery was filled with soft, dim beams of light that needled down from many small apertures in the ceiling.

"There she is," whispered the Professor.

"Rark! There who is?" Doris blinked her eyes as they adjusted to this new, softer lighting.

"Ah!" gasped Meltem.

"Quaaooo!" Brenda saw the figure in the alcove at the end of the gallery. The Wonder Camel's eyelashes tingled with curiosity.

"Artemis!" Jim said quietly.

In the alcove, gently lit in a pool of soft beams, stood the beautifully carved statue of the Goddess Artemis.

"She's as glorious as the famous statue in the museum at Selcuk, near Ephesus," Jim murmured, approaching the statue.

"Not surprising," said von Nozzel, "on account of the fact that she's the very same statue. W-w-we've borrowed her for six months for a temporary exhibition. There aren't many around as exquisite as She."

The Professor, Meltem, Brenda, and Doris (perched on Brenda's head, between the Wonder Camel's ears) followed Cairo Jim to Artemis. There they stood silently, admiring Her grace and majesty.

Her smooth marble face was as serene as the first ray of sunshine creeping from behind a cloud. Time had been good to Her; only a small chip of marble was missing from Her finely chiselled nose. Otherwise, the rest of Her features – Her strong but at the same time delicate jawline; Her high, polished cheekbones; Her steady and commanding eyes that gazed out through all of the dim Eternity before Her; Her kindly smile set into soft and gentle lips – were as perfect as the day they were carved.

Doris blinked and flexed herself up and down on Brenda's head (Brenda gave a soft watch-those-claws-my-little-friend type of snort). "Rark! That's some dress She's wearing!"

Indeed it was. The sculpted marble dress was full – almost bursting – with great plump fruit-shapes, from her neckline down to her waist. They looked like representations of eggs, or pomegranates, or aubergines, but whatever they were, there was no doubt about one thing: they suggested great abundance and copiousness.

"And check out that crown," Brenda thought-snorted.

As one, Jim, Doris, Meltem and the Professor gazed up at the towering crown on the statue's head. Three temples sat at the top of this crown, one on top of the other, all of them supported by small tiers of serious-looking griffins and serene-looking sphinxes.

"She is the oldest Goddess in the entire w-w-world," sighed Hieronymous von Nozzel, his voice filled with a long lifetime of great devotion to all things ancient.

"That She is," Jim said. "I remember your lectures as though it were only yesterday, Professor. You told us that the ancient Greeks worshipped Her as Artemis. To the older Anatolian civilisations, She was called Cybele. And the Romans, later on, knew Her as Diana."

"That's right, my boy." Von Nozzel gave a wrinkled

smile. "To all of them, She was the mighty, all-knowing Mother."

"Quaooo," snorted Brenda, her eyelashes tingling excitedly.

Meltem, standing close by Jim's shoulder, asked in a voice full of awe: "Professor, please tell us about Her Petticoat. And the Belt of Bountaiety."

"W-w-well," said von Nozzel, leaning on his walking stick, "to understand about that, I have to take you back in time. Back to the y-y-year AD 53."

"Just make sure we're back for lunch," chirped Doris.

"Sh, my dear," Jim winked at her.

The Professor gave her a stern but friendly look (as he had given many flippant students years earlier), and continued:

"The Great Goddess Artemis had been w-w-worshipped at Ephesus for more than one thousand years. Statues of Her, much like this one, decorated all the temples in the city, and Her image was to be found in every house and public square. She was known throughout the ancient w-w-world as 'Diana of the Ephesians', and travellers came from all corners of the globe to behold Her – the Mother Goddess – and Her mighty city."

Artemis looked down at Jim and the rest as von Nozzel continued. It was almost as if She were listening to the account with Her gentle, all-knowing smile.

"Then, in the y-y-year 53, St Paul brought the religion of Christianity to Ephesus. When he arrived at the

99

Temple of Artemis – one of the Seven Ancient W-w-wonders of the W-w-world, as you're no doubt aware – he was confronted by the towering statue of Artemis Herself, with Her face veiled and lamps burning at Her feet. Every altar throughout the city was burning lamps for Artemis. There was so much smoke from those lamps, in fact, that the entire city was smothered, and was dark, dark, dark.

"It took Paul and his followers a while to convince the Ephesians to get rid of Artemis and embrace the new religion. Around three hundred y-y-years, in fact. The reason why it took so long was largely because of the manufacturers of the Artemis statues, who stood to lose a lot of income from the change. But eventually things did change. The Christians branded Artemis a 'deceitful demon.' They took down the huge statue of Her from the centre of the town, and replaced it with Christ's victorious cross. Gradually the cult of Artemis was killed off.

"So it was that by the fourth century, long after the death of St Paul, the Christians had been so successful in denouncing Artemis that all mention of Her name had been smashed and scratched and obliterated from every inscription in Ephesus."

Doris blinked sadly and stretched her wings.

"But," continued Hieronymous von Nozzel, "let's go back a bit – to the second century. Here St John comes into the story and so, in effect, do w-w-*we*. According to the legend, St John converted the last of the Ephesians – some 40,000 of them – in a single day! What a day that was! Down at the Temple of Artemis the remaining

followers of Artemis threw open the doors, and Her choirs sang loudly in defiance. Huge clouds of incense blasted from inside the Temple, as if in a dying burst for something whose time had come.

"A couple of days later, St John's new followers descended in a violent frenzy upon the Temple of Artemis, ripping down the great statue and finally destroying the magnificent Temple. Column fell onto column, altars were smashed and shattered, inscriptions turned to powdery rubble by the force of their destruction. And so it was that the Temple of Artemis at Ephesus was no more."

Jim frowned and stared deeply into Artemis's bemused eyes.

"And here *our* story links up." Professor von Nozzel licked his old lips, his eyes moist with the telling of the story. "Like a baton being passed down through History, w-w-we have become part of the procession of the legend and the life of the Great Goddess Artemis. As I recounted in my book *At the End of the Deities*, there was at least one man who could not bear the destruction and the onslaught of enforced neglect that was taking place way back in the second century. Largely because of this man's deeds, the legend of Artemis has taken on a new meaning."

"Ancient deeds live on," said Jim of Cairo.

"Unfortunately," said the Professor, "because of this ancient man's noble actions, Neptune Bone has become a serious potential threat to the w-w-world..."

ANCIENT DEEDS NEVER DIE

"THE MAN'S NAME," said Professor von Nozzel, "was Caius Vibius Salutaris. He was a w-w-wealthy citizen of Ephesus who was alive fifty years after the death of St Paul, and he was an ardent and passionate w-w-worshipper of the cult of Artemis. Apart from the High Priests at the Temple, Salutaris was perhaps the most loyal to the Great Goddess, and his actions are proof of his devotion to Her.

"Caius Vibius Salutaris could not bear to see what was happening to Artemis in those early years of the Christian conversions. He found it horrible that She was being forced to leave Her city in such a barbaric fashion. We know so much because he left an inscription on a small marble slab, which was found in the 1960s by a group of Austrian archaeologists excavating some of the buildings at Ephesus."

Jim frowned. "The same archaeologists who discovered this statue?" he asked.

"The same," nodded von Nozzel.

"But that was an extremely famous discovery," Jim said, scratching his neck. "It was widely reported, and not only the statue, but all the other relics as

well. Yet I can't remember hearing about any marble inscription from Caius Vibius Salutaris."

"That's because it wasn't made public. The information on that inscription was too sensitive."

"Rerark!" Doris flexed herself impatiently up and down, opening her huge wings and folding them again. "What'd this inscription say?"

"And what," Meltem asked, "were these other relics found with the statue?"

Professor von Nozzel shifted his weight, and transferred his walking stick to his other hand. "I w-w-wish I had my copy of *At the End of the Deities* here with me," he sighed. "I wrote about it so w-w-well in that. Let me tell you: the Austrian team found this beautiful statue at the back of the Prytaneion – the Town Hall – at Ephesus. She was lying in a pit of fine sand, buried there – packed lovingly, you might say – by Caius Vibius Salutaris and his loyal staff. She had lain there for seventeen centuries, undisturbed by the passage of Time."

"And we know it was Salutaris who placed her there because of the inscription he left?" Jim asked.

"Y-y-yes," nodded von Nozzel.

"What'd it say? What'd it say?" Doris was squawking loudly.

"Before I answer your question, Doris, let me answer Meltem's. The other relics I spoke of? Oh, these were w-w-wonderful! Salutaris also rescued a number of items of the actual clothing and jewellery which used to

adorn Her statue. It was a common practice in those days to dress these great votive statues in clothing the same as that carved on the statue itself."

Meltem raised a shapely eyebrow. "I had no idea, Professor."

"Oh, y-y-yes. During antiquity, Artemis used to be dressed in garments made of very valuable fabrics. Only Her face and arms were ever exposed. The Austrians found, in the fine cushion of sand, two great leather belts, exactly the same as those two you can see carved onto the figure. They found a tall, majestic crown, made of silk w-w-woven with heavy gold thread, exactly like the one there in marble – with the three Ionic temples on it, and those griffins and sphinxes carrying those arches, embroidered onto the other tiers."

"Exquisite," whispered Meltem, and Brenda gave a snort of deep admiration.

"There was more that Salutaris packed away." Von Nozzel's eyes were moist with pleasure. "They found Her jewellery, protected in that soft sand: Her necklaces, dripping with amber from the Baltic, brilliant glass beads from Phoenicia, and dazzling crystal; small, intricate golden brooches in the likenesses of bees; magnificent lion-headed golden ornaments that were still sewn onto Her shawl, which was made of the finest silk. All of these were in perfect condition, as though they had been made only y-y-yesterday.

"But there w-w-were two items that the Austrian archaeologists didn't find. These two relics had been

w-w-whisked away by Caius Vibius Salutaris, and hidden in two different locations in ancient Turkey: the Sacred Petticoat of Artemis, with its plentiful folds and enigmatic pleatings, and the silver-and-gold Belt of Bountaiety, which went around it."

"Rark. He said so in his inscription, didn't he?" guessed Doris.

"That he did, Doris. He also told us why he was removing these two valuable items. Y-y-you see, his faith in Artemis was so strong that he could not bear the thought that these sacred relics might fall into the hands of non-believers, and Her power be diminished and lost for all of Eternity to neglect and indifference."

"Her power?" repeated Jim. "What sort of power?"

"According to Salutaris' inscription on the marble slab – which the Austrians quickly took back to their country after I had transcribed it, and where it remains locked away in a secret location – the Belt of Bountaiety is necessary to activate the awesome power that Artemis had Herself invested into the Sacred Petticoat."

"Quaoooo?" snorted Brenda, a flicker of worry darting through her mane.

"The inscription said that whosoever w-w-wore the Sacred Petticoat of the Great Goddess Artemis, *with the Belt of Bountaiety around the w-w-waist of the garment*, would have all the untold powers of Artemis Herself."

"Well swoggle me sweetly," gasped Cairo Jim.

"You mean...?" whispered Meltem.

"The w-w-wearer of the garments," said Hieronymous von Nozzel, "could bring forth life and abundance, could make the barren fertile, and change the very courses of nature!"

"Wait just a moment!" Jim looked deep into the Eternity-glimpsing face of Artemis. "If the wearer of the Petticoat could do all that, then is it possible they could also do the opposite? That they could take the life away from a place, and make it worthless? That they could be in control of the whole ruination of somewhere?"

"That," answered the Professor, "is something w-w-we have never had to contend with."

"Until now," said Jim gravely. An enormous rush of dread swept over him. "We have to stop this bloated wretch, and quickly!"

"Y-y-you need to get the Belt of Bountaiety to do that," von Nozzel said. "Bone's got the Petticoat, but it's not any use to him w-w-without the Belt."

"Where do we look, Professor?" asked Doris.

"Aphrodisias," he answered. "According to Salutaris' inscription, he hid the Belt of Bountaiety somewhere in the ancient ruins at Aphrodisias. W-w-where exactly, we do not know. But he had his helpers carve another inscription somewhere on one of the buildings there, which will lead you to the Belt's w-w-whereabouts."

"Let's hope this building is still standing, or at least the part of it that bears the information," Meltem said.

"We haven't an inkling of a second to waste," announced Jim. "Bone's probably halfway there already." He took Brenda's bridle and began leading her out of the gallery. "We'll do our best, Professor. Thank you for your information. Hopefully we'll have this Belt for you very soon."

"Y-y-yes ... may all y-y-your luck be of the highest and most virtuous order," he said, watching them leave.

"If you need to contact us," called Meltem, "telephone me care of the Antiquities Squad in Istanbul. They will pass on your message." She disappeared through the doorway, and Jim gave the Professor a wave before ushering Doris and Brenda out.

Alone in the dim gallery, Professor Hieronymous von Nozzel listened as their echoing foot- and hoof-steps faded off into the distance. He felt a chill across his shoulders, and he blinked behind his thick spectacles.

The Belligerent Serpent of Antiocheia, he suddenly remembered. *I didn't warn them about the Belligerent Serpent of Antiocheia!*

He covered his mouth with his parchment-like hand, and took a deep breath. "No," he said aloud to the empty gallery. "No, it is best not to w-w-worry them with legend at this point in their quest. If *legend* is all it is..."

The chill came again, colder and faster, this time rushing down his back. He turned to see the Great Goddess Artemis smiling benignly down at him. Then he gave a shiver – a big, chilled shiver – and slowly hobbled out of the gallery and back to his room.

Part Two:

THE THREAT
OF PLENTY

APHRODISIAS

THE EARLY MORNING sunlight bathed the ruins of Aphrodisias in a golden, almost dazzling, serenity.

"Rerark!" squawked Doris, who was waddling about on top of a truncated column. "What a beautiful place! You can almost feel Time staying still, can't you?"

Cairo Jim, busy inspecting the marble steps of the nearby remains of the Temple of Aphrodite with his Perspicacity-brand Archaeological Magnifying Glass, smiled. "You can, my dear, you can."

"It's as though it's been locked away from the rest of the world, it's so calm and peaceful. Rark."

Brenda gave a snort and lowered her snout to remove a scraggly wad of grass and weeds that was covering a marble slab near her hoofs. She felt the sunlight seeping into her humps, and it made her eyelashes tingle in a very agreeable sort of way.

A small, soft breeze blew down from the distant, snow-capped mountains. Meltem put on her sun-spectacles and went to join Jim, who was crouching on the steps of the Temple. "Do you have any idea," she asked him in a voice full of respect and as warm as the sunshine), "where we might find the inscription of Caius Vibius Salutaris?"

"Could be anywhere, Meltem," he answered, squinting at the worn and scratched marble.

"You must call me Mel. Please."

He looked up at her and smiled. "So much of this place has fallen down, or been pulled apart. Salutaris' inscription might be on some of the columns or walls that are still standing, or it might be on a bit of masonry or a slab that's on the ground, overgrown with grass and covered with earth and goodness knows what."

"Well," she said, rolling up the sleeves of her chic but practical field jacket (she had persuaded Jim, Doris and Brenda to stop for a few minutes at her apartment in Istanbul when they had left the Museum, so that she could change her clothes). "Let's get cracking, shall we?"

Doris flexed herself up and down. "This inscription could be lurking right beneath our very beak, noses and snout! Betcha I find it first!"

Brenda gave a not-if-I'm-a-Wonder-Camel-you-won't snort and lowered her head to the overgrown slabs.

"At least we have a fine day ahead of us," said Jim, setting his jaw determinedly and carefully inspecting the marble.

At the Pera Palas Hotel, Neptune Bone was stirred from his half-slumber by a shrill-voiced messenger bursting into the Coco Chanel Manicure Salon.

"Urgent package for Mr Impluvium!" whined the young man, his voice sounding like the cry of a small furry animal caught in a food blender. "Urgent package for Mr Impluvium!"

Bone's eyes shot open, and he sat upright. The seven manicurists and three foot masseurs who had been attending to him all moved silently out of his way as he lurched to his feet.

"I'll have that," he sneered, and snatched the buff-coloured envelope from the youth's hand.

"Arrr," he murmured. He puffed gloatingly on his cigar as he tore open the envelope and beheld the fat wad of land deeds that were wedged tightly inside. "Another stage closer to my forthcoming state of Greatness."

The messenger stood with his hand extended, waiting for a tip. "Aher-aherm," he said (this time sounding like a cross between someone clearing his throat and a steam train hitting the brakes all too suddenly).

Bone looked at the youth, then at the open hand. With a flabby wink of his eyelid, Bone ashed his cigar into the messenger's palm.

"Yeeoooowwww!" The young man shook his hand about wildly, shoved it under the armpit of his tunic, and swiftly left the Salon.

"Singed by grandeur," remarked the fleshy man. He plonked his fez onto his greasy hair and clicked his fingers. "Desdemona! Come! We must hit the road to my bright and glorious future! Arrrrrrrrrr."

"Aye, aye, my Captain," came the raven's muffled croak. She hop-fluttered from the cupboard full of expensive perfumes, where, unbeknown to the world, she had been treating herself to far too much of the finer things in life.

The afternoon passed quickly, and soon the sun was beginning its descent behind the distant mountains. Aphrodisias was becoming washed in the soft, golden glow of twilight.

Despite the steady inspection of the ruins by Jim, Doris, Brenda and Meltem, the inscription of Caius Vibius Salutaris had yet to reveal itself.

"Maybe this is it," squawked Doris, one eye closed as she squinted at a scratchy message on a fragment of ancient tombstone. She cleared her throat and read aloud: 'Beuchychin's mother is a walrus'."

Cairo Jim looked up from the marble slabs he was dusting. "No, my dear, I think that's more graffiti."

"Hrmph," hrmphed the macaw. "That's all we've come across all afternoon. Graffiti and graffiti and graffiti. Modern-day vandalism, the lot of it. Outrageous!"

"Quaaaooo," snorted Brenda, running her sensitive nostrils across a fallen plinth that lay half-covered by tall grasses. Like Doris, she, too, had found many examples of this sort of vandalism during the last few hours.

Doris arched her crestfeathers indignantly forward. "Who cares if Beuchychin's mother's a walrus? Or if Drusilla and Norman were here in 1973? Or if Shirley Bassey rules? Or if some moron with a sharp implement wanted to tell the world his opinions on the World Cup? Rark! Human beings have no respect for the past!"

"Not *all* human beings," Jim gently reminded her.

She blinked and lifted her wings. With a fluid swish of her beautiful feathers, she fluttered to Jim's side, and nuzzled her beak against his hand. "My apologies," she prerked. "I would never include you in that round-up of disrespect."

The archaeologist-poet tousled her plumage and smiled. "But you're right, Doris. Many humans have no idea how acts such as these help to destroy the mighty past."

Meltem popped her head up from behind a segment of a stone altar. "It is awful that this vandalism is happening in my country. I wish it were otherwise."

Jim smiled at her, and she returned the smile in an embarrassed sort of way.

Brenda raised her neck and peered up at the mountains. The last rays of direct sunlight were now spearing up from behind the peaks, shooting out in all directions like colossal, spindly, golden fingers. *"It's getting late,"* the Wonder Camel thought. *"Soon the light will be too weak to continue searching."*

Jim took off his pith helmet and wiped the back of his neck. "It's getting late," he said quietly. "Soon the light will be too weak to continue searching."

"Rark. Let's set up camp. Bren and I can go and find some wood for a fire, can't we, Bren?"

"Quaaoooo."

"Good idea," Meltem said. She took off her sun-spectacles and looked around. "How about we settle down for the night over there, by the Portico of Tiberius?"

Cairo Jim smiled at her choice. It seemed like just the place to spend the night.

Two hours later, the campfire was blazing steadily and warmly, and Jim was cooking a large pot of vegetable soup. On the road to Aphrodisias they had bought vegetables and some fresh, crusty bread; Jim often made soup when camping, and Doris and Brenda had come to look forward to his special concoctions, which had grown more delicious over time.

Meltem sat on the ground, comfortable on Jim's camp blanket and leaning against Brenda's macramé saddle. She watched Jim as he stirred the soup, and she felt herself warming by the glow of the fire. Slowly she undid her bun and let her long, shiny hair fall loose about her shoulders.

Doris had her pack of cards out and was trying to interest Brenda in a game of gin rummy, but the Wonder Camel had other ideas. Being a creature who slept very little during the night, she wanted to keep searching for the ancient inscription, using her nostrils as her guide.

Doris gave up trying to persuade Brenda, and waddled across to see if she could give Jim some advice on the soup instead.

"Yes, my dear, I've added the pepper."

"Rark. Is there celery in it?"

"Yes. And carrots."

She blinked in an approving sort of way.

"You know something?" Meltem said.

"What, Meltem?" asked Jim.

"Mel. Please, Jim."

"What, Mel?"

She stretched her legs out so her feet were closer to the fire. "I'm surprised that Bone has not arrived here by now. I would have thought he'd have come straight away to try and obtain the Belt."

"He's lazy," Jim said. "He probably hasn't even read the Professor's book yet. Or maybe he *has* read it..."

Meltem raised a shapely eyebrow.

"He's also the most calculating and devious man I've known," Jim went on. "He may have read the book, he may already know exactly where he's supposed to be searching. But he might be laying low ... staying out of the way for a while so that the Antiquities Squad will lose interest."

Meltem sat forward and pulled her knees up so they were under her chin. "Jim of Cairo," she smiled, her dark eyes seeming even darker and more fathomless in the dancing light of the fire, "I'll have you know that once we have our sights set on someone, we members of the Antiquities Squad *never* lose interest."

"Hmmm," thought Doris at the smooth, honey-like way Meltem said that.

Across the ruins, in the strong light from the three-quarter moon, Brenda was snorting quietly about in the rubble.

She was using the intricate muscles of her Wonder Camel nostrils to carefully feel her way across the flat surfaces of stone lying in the grass before her. Other muscles in her snout she had shut off, so that any ancient dust would not be inhaled. (Sneezing was an activity that all Wonder Camels tried to avoid whenever possible – it had a nasty hump-tingling effect which was no fun at all, and could, in the worst cases, lead to temporary amnesia.)

So strong was her concentration on the task at hand that she did not detect the silent movement of a car's headlights as they swung across the hillside next to her.

Nor did she hear the soft, steady purr of a Bugatti's motor coming closer and closer through the night...

13

THE SLITHERING PAST

"ARRR! NEXT TIME we visit a prestige hotel such as what the Pera Palas is, I absolutely forbid you to go anywhere near the perfumery cupboard. My eyes haven't stopped watering since we left Istanbul!"

Desdemona sat on the top of the Bugatti's passenger seat, staring straight and throbbingly ahead into the darkness, the pores beneath her feathers oozing with a vile combination of sweet smells. "I think I have achieved a unique aroma," she croaked proudly.

"You've achieved an abomination of stinkiness, that's what you've achieved." Bone wiped his eyes with a lacy silk handkerchief that had once belonged to his mother, and steered the car round a bend in the road. "What fragrances did you squirt upon yourself, you tasteless trollop of tackiness?"

"Only one or two," answered the raven, who had never been able to count properly.

"Which one or two? I shall have them banned globally when I rule the world."

"Let's see ... there was *Compost d'Amour*, then *Rhapsody of Rhubarb*. I squirted that behind this wing. Then I tried one called *Le Petite Poopoo*, followed by *Poisson Mystère* and a touch of *Musky Adventure*.

Oh, and then I dabbed on a bit of *Shocking* by Schiaperilli under my tarsus. Here, have a sniff."

"Keep your tailfeathers away from me, Desdemona!"

"Suit yourself. And finally, I found a bottle right at the back of the cupboard. What was that one called? Oh, yeah. *Nuance of Ammonia.* I poured quite a bit of that on my tummy feathers. That was a mistake, that one – the fleas seem to like it."

Bone rolled his watering eyes and shook his head slowly. "Of all the idiotic, pea-brained, amoeba-stupid birds – *oh, by the Goddess Betsy, look, Desdemona!*"

He hit the brakes, snapped off the headlights, and moved his wide face closer to the windscreen.

"What?" she grunted, picking herself up from the floor. She hopped back onto the top of the passenger seat. "What's the sudden—?"

"Shhh! Keep it low! Look, out there."

Ahead, by a small hillside and a dozen derelict marble columns, with her mane lit up by the steady moonlight, Brenda was sniffing assiduously through the ancient remnants.

"A camel," said the raven quietly. "So what? I saw lotsa camels down near Ephesus. Turkey's full of 'em."

"Not just any camel," Bone purred, his fleshy lips curling into a smile. "Look at the extra-long eyelashes on that one. That's that ruminant quadruped who hangs around with that goody-goody gumbum, Cairo Jim. The dreadful dromedary herself!"

"Crark!"

"And, judging from the earnestness that is rippling through her moonlit mane, she is searching for something." He turned to Desdemona and his voice went all thin. "I'd bet my last fez they're onto us, and that humped monstrosity is looking for the inscription of Caius Vibius Salutaris that we read about in the Professor's book."

Desdemona watched Brenda through slitted eyes. "The one that shows the way to the Belt of Bountaiety?"

"The very same. Arrrr."

"Oooh oooh oooh!"

"What's wrong – has a flea gone down the wrong way again?"

"No, no, no. I just had a thought!"

"And they said the days of miracles were past."

"Now's our chance, my Captain. If Brenda the Wonder Camel is here, then Jim of Cairo and that gaudy, chatterbox show-off of a macaw, Doris, will be nearby as well. Let's go and finish 'em off!" She raised one leg into the air and arched her talons menacingly.

Bone watched Brenda as his mind turned over Desdemona's suggestion. The Wonder Camel was searching very slowly, her nostrils exploring every millimetre before her. Her nostril muscles were the only part of her moving – her head and body were so still that she could have been an ancient statue, serene and remote in the night.

"No," Bone answered presently. "I have a better plan. One thing I have learned, through my ongoing procession of Extreme Genius, is this: there is no point in working hard for your goals when there are others there to do the work for you. Why should I chip any of my valuable and beautiful fingernails when others are already snouting around in the dirt?"

Desdemona gave him a sideways look.

"Let us pull over, and park our Bugatti behind those bushes, where we can keep a careful eye on the humped huntress over there. Then, when she has found the inscription – maybe even the Belt of Bountaiety itself – we will move in, and remove not only her, but also Jim and the flying feather duster with whom he keeps company."

"Remove them?" croaked the bird.

"Once and finally. I have always felt that the world was not a fitting place for such misguided and idiotic niceness. Arrrrrrrrrrr!"

What I am looking for, Brenda thought deeply, *is a single Latin letter. That was the alphabet in which Caius Vibius Salutaris would have written his message, because that was the language used in Ephesus in Roman times.*

She didn't know what that letter would be ... maybe a D or a V or a C. Maybe not even one of those. But she knew that once she found a single letter of the type used in the ancient Roman script, then she would probably find other letters. Maybe they would be right next to the first letter she would find, or maybe, if the slab containing the first letter had smashed, the other letters would be on nearby fragments of marble in the grass. If that was the case, then Jim and Doris and she would have an ancient jigsaw puzzle to piece together.

As her sensitive nostrils moved across the marble, she concentrated – as hard as she had concentrated on anything before – and in her mind she began to see the curves and straight lines that made up the letters of the Latin alphabet.

Carefully, with her unique Wonder Camel precision of mind, muscle and minutiae, she transferred the images in her head to the muscles of her nostrils.

This marble slab was cool against her snout: cool and hard. It was also flat and smooth and, as she concentrated to the minutest of degrees, Brenda could tell that it was uninscribed. There were no human-made markings carved into this stone, no vestiges of Latin anywhere.

She shut her eyes and slowly moved her head to the left, still keeping her nostrils close to the ground. Now she felt small prickles of grass-blades brushing past, some of them furry and some of them sharp. Quickly she moved her head further to the left.

She opened her eyes suddenly. The hairs around her nostrils had struck another slab of marble, and the cool, smooth surface came as a nice change from the grass. She opened her eyes and inspected this new slab.

This slab was lying under the branches of an ancient, gnarled tree, and the leaves and branches of the tree shut out the rays of the moon. Brenda found it was much darker here, too dark to accurately see that which was underhoof. She flared her nostrils and started to read through her nose again.

A thick layer of dirt and dust blanketed the slab. Brenda took a deep breath, then blew the air out of her mouth as hard as she could, at the same time clamping her nostrils shut. A big cloud of grit shot out from the slab.

When the dust settled, she put her nostrils back to the task. Nothing on the top of the slab, only cool, smooth marble. She moved her head down along the length of the stone.

Nothing midway along the slab, except for a slight bump that rippled across the middle of the rock. Probably just a natural imperfection in the marble, Brenda thought.

Slowly she moved her snout to the bottom end.

And then, just before she came to the lower edge, her nostrils felt something!

A shape. A curve. Joined to a straight line. Small, but clearly chiselled into the stone, about five millimetres deep.

The Roman letter D.

Brenda moved her nostrils infinitesimally to the right, and there, neatly spaced, was another shape. Another letter. A single line, the same height as the D.

To the right of this, spaced at the same distance, was a third shape: a curve and a neat straight line.

Brenda's nostrils recognised it immediately as a G.

With a great surge of excitement rippling through her mane and further back along her humps, the Wonder Camel continued her snout-deciphering:

DIG BENEATH. HERE LIES THE SACRED BUCKLE OF
THE GREAT GODDESS ARTEMIS, ALL-KNOWING MOTHER,
SHE WHOSE GREATNESS FOREVERMORE BE REMEMBERED.
I, CAIUS VIBIUS SALUTARIS, A HUMBLE WORSHIPPER, LAID
THIS STONE. REUNITE THIS BUCKLE OF ABUNDANCE
WITH HER BELT OF BOUNTAIETY, HIDDEN IN THE
UNDERGROUND CITY OF K

And there the slab of marble finished in a jagged, broken fracture.

The clever Wonder Camel raised her head, gave a loud snort, and lowered her snout to try and find the rest of the inscription.

So absorbed was she in what she had come across, and what she was hoping to find, that she didn't notice the change in texture beneath her nostrils. First there had been dirt, then smooth coolness again.

But this smooth coolness was different to the smooth coolness of all the marble she had been inspecting. That had all been dry, after she had cleared it of the dust and grit of the past centuries. This place she was snouting was not dry. In fact, there was an altogether distinct clamminess here.

Brenda continued moving her snout across the area under her. The darkness was still heavy here; the branches of the ancient tree seemed to spread as though they would never end. Not even the faintest beam of moonshimmer penetrated through.

Sniiiiffffff. Brenda shook her head. Was that a bead of moisture that had shot up her nose?

She blinked and then snorted quietly. Yes, it was, and it had a pungent, sickly smell to it, a smell that was now seeping down into her taste buds.

She lowered her head again to what she thought was the marble slab she'd been inspecting. With quivering nostrils, she discovered that the entire area under her snout was not marble, but something else.

Something clammy and – could it be? – *pulsating.*

Her head shot up, and she snorted wildly and loudly for Jim and Doris. Her alarm travelled across Aphrodisias like a spreading pool of fear.

QUUUUAAAAOOOOOOOOOOOOO!

The ground beneath her groaned and stirred. Slabs of marble that had been lying still on the earth began to slide and shift.

Behind Brenda, near the base of the tree, a long, pointed wedge of sliminess speared up through the ground and whipped loudly against the gnarled tree trunk.

And there, not five metres from Brenda's snout, an enormous eye opened in the ground.

"Reeeaaaark! Jim, it's Bren!"

Cairo Jim jumped up from the fire. "Where, Doris? Which direction?"

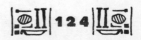

"That way!" She flew to his arm.

"Let's go," Meltem urged.

"Follow me!" shouted the archaeologist-poet, flashing his torch into the ruins ahead.

The Belligerent Serpent of Antiocheia had been written about as far back as the second century. According to legend, the Serpent roamed ceaselessly under the most ancient layers of earth. Many people refused to believe in the Serpent, but those who regularly spent lonely hours watching sheep amongst the old, crumbled towns in these parts treated the legendary beast with great respect.

Now, before Brenda's wide, unblinking eyes, the Serpent was rearing up from beneath the soil, pushing aside great slabs of what had once been the Tetrapylon – the monumental gateway – of Aphrodisias. Its huge scaly back arched upwards, like a steep bridge.

Slowly Brenda began to rise, higher and higher still, her hoofs straining to stay firm on the slimy scales underneath. She shut her eyes and tried not to squeal.

Stay calm, she told herself. *Panic will get you nowhere.*

Up and up she continued, her hoofs sliding uncontrollably. Now she was the height of two humans above the ground. Then, with a great rippling, the movement stopped.

Silence.

And another sound...

Brenda heard a low, guttural hissing in front of her.

Gulping the terror deep down into her throat, she opened her eyes.

There, three metres below her, a gigantic, wrinkled head stared with dark, never-see-the-light eyes. Beneath the eyes, a wide mouth was opening slowly.

Suddenly a beam of light shot under the tree as Jim flashed his torch at the scene. He, Doris and Meltem stopped, stunned in their tracks.

"The Belligerent Serpent of Antiocheia," gasped Meltem. "It must be!"

Jim's light shone into the Serpent's chasm of a mouth, and everyone saw the countless rows of razor-sharp, green-mouldy fangs protruding in a twisted tangle of ghastliness.

The hairs in Brenda's mane stood on end, and her hoofs gave way and began to slip.

"Brenda!" cried Jim. "*No!*"

"She's sliding towards its mouth!" screeched Doris.

Meltem shut her eyes.

Brenda's hoofs scrabbled all around the dripping purple and green scales, trying to gain purchase. But it was no good – the harder she tried to find a grip, the slipperier everything became.

The Serpent opened its mouth wider, wider, as Brenda slipped closer, closer...

Cairo Jim shuddered – this was all happening so fast, there was no time to think. No time to react. Surely such a brave and noble creature as Brenda would not end up like—

"*QUAAAOOOOOOOOO!*" Brenda snorted with all the urgency she had ever felt. She pushed out telepathically, like she had never pushed out telepathically before, and sent a message to the Serpent, hoping that it would understand her thoughts:

"I come with no threat to you. I come in the name of protecting the past!"

Over and over Brenda pushed out the message. *"Protecting the past, protecting the past!"*

Now she was only centimetres from the Serpent's fangs. She felt the stale, hot breath of the creature, and the low, steady hissing filled her Wonder Camel ears. *"I come with no threat"* – her thought-message almost screamed out of her head – *"I come in the name of protecting the past!"*

And the creature closed its eyes, lowered its back, and slowly set Brenda down.

"That is underssssstood," came a hiss that only Brenda heard the meaning behind.

"Raaark," screeched Doris, her feathers trembling. "It's putting her down!"

Jim shone his torch at the head of the Serpent.

"Look," he whispered. "There, in amongst all those furrows above its eyes. It's some sort of..."

Brenda watched as the Belligerent Serpent of Antiocheia lowered its massive head before her. It gave another hiss, this one loud and long like steam escaping from some colossal kettle. Brenda listened to the hiss and interpreted the meaning behind it:

"I have waited here for many centuriesssss. It hasssss been my duty to protect thisssss. My time of protection hasssss finished. Now I hand it to you, for it wasssss to be that there would come a Protector of the power of Artemisssss. Have what I have had, and leave me."

A deep ripple passed through the many furrows above the Serpent's eyes, and the wrinkles there flattened out until they had almost disappeared. From amid the wrinkles, where it had lain for longer than Aphrodisias had been ruins, a large silver object fell.

It dropped silently to the grass before Brenda's hoofs. She looked down at it, and then into the eyes of the Serpent, which were no longer darker than the longest night. Now there were tiny beads of colour in them, like stars appearing in the sky.

"The Buckle of Abundance," hissed the Belligerent Serpent of Antiocheia.

"Quaooo," snorted Brenda quietly.

The Serpent lowered its head, and Brenda lowered hers. Then, without any hissing or ceremony, the ancient, legendary Serpent laid itself against the earth and the grasses and the slabs of bygone civilisations, and in five seconds it had flattened itself completely, to become part of all that was around it.

"It's gone," gasped Doris. "Disappeared entirely!"

"Come on," said Jim, "let's see what it left Brenda!"

14

TO THE UNDERGROUND...

"THUS IT IS THAT THE PAST unfurls its secrets," murmured Neptune Bone, his eyes still wide at the scene he had just witnessed. "Arrrr."

"Bleccch," winced Desdemona. "Snakes! I need snakes like another million fleas!"

"Shut up, you abominable aggregation of aromas, time is not to be wasted here. Look, there in the gloom of that tree. Cairo Jim and his raven and some person of the female persuasion have joined the camel. Quickly, Desdemona, narrow your eyes. Fly into the dark branches of that tree and eavesdrop on them all. Find out what they're up to."

"Leavesdrop? What good'd that do? Leaves won't hurt 'em. Why don't I drop *bricks* on 'em? Bricks'd bruise 'em good. Or toasters? Or bits of ancient cement? Leaves wouldn't even stun a fly!"

"Not leavesdrop, you feathered fool! *Eavesdrop.* Listen in on their conversation. And then report back to me, pronto pronto." He swiped her away with his fez.

"Crark, I go, I go, I go."

"And stay in the darkest places," he hissed after her. He rested his bulbous nose on the steering wheel

and stared ahead. "For it is in the darkest places that our destiny lies," he purred knowingly to himself.

"A buckle?" said Doris.

Brenda held the Buckle of Abundance in her jaws. Jim put out his hand, and she let it drop into his palm.

"I wonder," he said slowly, "if this is part of the Belt?"

"Rark. What do you reckon, Meltem?"

She frowned. "I'm afraid I have no idea."

Brenda gave a look-where-I-am-showing-you snort, and scraped a hoof across the marble slab that had slipped onto its side with the rising of the Belligerent Serpent of Antiocheia.

"What's that, my lovely?"

Doris jumped down from Jim's shoulder and waddled speedily to the marble. "Rerk, Bren's found an inscription!"

"Well swoggle me by Salutaris," whispered Jim. He shone his beam at the marble slab. "Look, see the pattern of egg-shapes carved all around the border? We've heard about those. Remember? Professor von Nozzel said the casket containing the Petticoat had an egg-shaped border around the lid."

He and Meltem went and crouched by the Latin writing.

They were all silent for a few moments, while Jim's torch illuminated the message. The only sound was a muffled whooshing in the branches above them, but nobody below heard it, so engrossed were they in the inscription.

"The Buckle of Abundance," Doris read aloud.

"So it *is* connected to the Belt," said Cairo Jim at last.

"Not now it isn't," corrected Doris. "We've got to get to some underground city of K. That's where we'll find the Belt."

"Not K," Meltem said. "See, the slab is broken after the first letter of the name. I am certain that Salutaris had the whole name inscribed there: Kaymaklı."

Above, the raven committed the name Kaymaklı to her memory.

"It is the largest underground city in Turkey," Meltem explained. "We call these underground cities Yeralti Sehris. They were built by the Troglodytes, who lived in them when there was danger of battle. The city at Kaymaklı was established almost 4000 years ago."

Jim's eyeballs felt furry, a sure sign that his excitement levels were rising. He had read about the Yeralti Sehris, and had always hoped that one day he'd have the chance to explore them himself.

"Where is Kaymaklı?" he asked Meltem.

"To the east, just south of the city of Nevsehir. Probably about six hundred kilometres from here. We will travel through the Valleys of the Fairy Chimneys in Cappadocia to get there."

"How long do you think it'll take?" asked the archaeologist-poet. "I'm not familiar with the roads and byways here."

Meltem pushed back a lock of her lustrous hair and smiled at Brenda. "With her strong and fast hoofs, I'd say that if we leave at daybreak we would be there by early afternoon tomorrow."

"Quaaooo," snorted Brenda. She was relieved that there would be some time for rest before they set out – the appearance of the Serpent had exhausted her.

Jim put the Buckle of Abundance into one of his shirt pockets, and buttoned down the pocket-flap. "Right. Time for some shut-eye." He turned to go back to the campfire, then stopped.

Meltem noticed him twitching his nose. At once she couldn't help thinking how he resembled a small rabbit when he did that. "Is there anything wrong, Jim?" she asked, in almost the sort of voice she would be using if he *were* a small rabbit.

"Can anyone smell something sweet?" he asked. "Something almost sickly?"

The branches above stirred. There was a sudden glint of moonlight, and then the return of darkness.

"It's gone now," Jim said, still wrinkling his nose. "For a few seconds it was as strong as an ox. Erck!"

"Probably just the lingering presence of the Serpent," squawked Doris, fluttering back to his arm. "C'mon, buddy-boy, Brenda needs some rest."

"Arrr, so tell me: what are they up to? Have they got the Belt?"

Desdemona's eyeballs throbbed redly as she perched

on top of the windscreen. "Well, they've found themselves this big silver thing called the Buckle of Ablunderance—"

"The Buckle of Ablunderance?"

"—which has to be connected to the Belt."

"Yes?" Bone puffed impatiently on a Belch of Brouhaha. "Yes, yes, yes? Where is the Belt?"

"Not here." She pecked savagely at a mass of fleas who were using her back as a trampoline-cum-smorgasbord.

"Not here? Then where?"

"The hideous humped one found a bit of marble that's got some writing on it. The writing said that the Belt could be found in some underground city."

"Did it have a name, this underground city?"

"Yep, the woman knew it. Let me see ... began with a K. K. K, K, K. K something..."

"Kaymaklı?" sneered Bone.

"Crark, that's it! Howd'd ya know?"

"It's the biggest underground city in Turkey. I have always kept it in mind as a possible place to lay low when those wretches from the Antiquities Squad are breathing a little too close down my neck for comfort. One could hide in there for years without being discovered, if one wanted to."

"Apparently we have to travel through some valleys of fairy chilblains in a cappuccino to get there."

Bone rolled his eyes. "That's Cappadocia, you misinformed mutant. And they're not fairy chilblains, they're—oh, why do I bother?"

"Jim and his pathetic posse are leaving at daybreak. They want to get some rest first. Crark! That gives us a head start, whaddya say?"

"I say no, Desdemona."

"No?"

"No." He reached forward and ashed his cigar into her eyes. She blinked, then blinked again. Then she blinked a third time. Then she made a noise like a car horn with the hiccups.

"No, we shall give *them* the head start." Bone reached over into the back seat, and lifted the silver casket containing the Sacred Petticoat of Artemis. He placed the casket carefully on his knees, and ran his hands delicately across the gold egg motifs on the lid.

"Why?" asked Desdemona, blinking the ashes from her eyes.

"Because, as I said before, it is much more brilliant to let others do the work for you. The underground city of Kaymaklı is a treacherous and uncertain place, I happen to know. Why should anything bad or disastrous happen to us, when it could just as easily happen to them?"

The edges of the raven's beak curled into a fiendish leer.

"And," Bone continued in a sardonic whisper, "death by misadventure – the accidental and mysterious disappearance of an archaeologist-poet and his awful entourage, after they have discovered the Belt of Bountaiety, of course – will be much less suspicious, don't you think?" He tilted his head back, his eyes glinting in the moonlight. "This way, I shall achieve my Plan of Genius and finally eliminate my nemesis, all without barely having to lift a finger."

"Misadventure! Craaark!"

Bone caressed the casket lid, his pudgy hands warm with the thrill of what was to come. "How sweet life is when fortune and myself walk hand-in-hand along the promenade of dreams. *Arrrrrrrrrrrrrrr.*"

15

MELTEM CHANGES HER TUNE

THE SOFT RAYS OF THE DAWN sun wavered down through the trees, tinting the columns and fallen walls and the still, silent statues and sarcophaguses of Aphrodisias with a weak, honey-coloured light.

"Doris!" whispered Jim. "My dear, time to stir!"

Above, perched on a tree branch, the macaw jerked her wings and opened her eyes. She blinked heavily and peered down at him.

"We have to go very soon," he said, raising his arm.

"Rark, am I glad you woke me." She stretched her wings and swooped down to land atop his bent elbow. "Had the strangest dream about lambs. There were all these lambs, all dancing around in a circle, and they were all spouting poetry!"

"Poetry?"

"Mm-hm. All sorts of poetry: love poetry, silly poetry, odes to Grecian urns and mermaids, poems that you wouldn't want to read on Get Well cards. And then they all stopped dancing round in a circle, and they all looked at me with their lamb eyes wide and their woolly bits all aquiver. And they said a final poem, loudly and bleatingly." Doris lowered her voice and recited it slowly:

"'Don't rely on Meltem's phone,
Cairo Jim, you're on your own,
don't leave any unturned stone,
GET THE BELT – THWART NEPTUNE
BONE!'"

"Hmmm," said Jim, starting to pack his knapsack.

"And do you know what these lambs called themselves?" asked Doris.

"What, my dear?"

"The Rhyming Cutlets. Erk!"

Meltem emerged from behind the ancient altar of the Temple of Aphrodite, where she had been brushing her hair and tying it into a bun. "I could not help overhearing," she smiled. "I, too, had strange dreams last night. I dreamt that Bone was close to me – very close – and his eyes were like the eyes of the Belligerent Serpent of Antiocheia. And he was wrapping his tail around me, squeezing and..." Her face clouded, and she turned away.

"It was only a nightmare," Jim said. "I often have them when we're camping at ancient places. I think it's something to do with the past still being here, like a force that can't seep away. When we're asleep and not alert, the things from the past come in, as though we've opened a door into our souls."

Meltem turned back to him. "You are a thoughtful and clever man, Jim of Cairo. Two qualities which many people underestimate."

The archaeologist-poet blushed and quickly put on

his sun-spectacles. Then he busied himself with the straps on Brenda's saddlebags.

"When you two have finished with your meeting of the Cairo Jim Appreciation Society," said Doris, waddling around impatiently, "we can saddle up Brenda and be off! The day is getting up and leaving us behind!"

At the sound of her name, the Wonder Camel ambled into the clearing and gently nuzzled Jim in the back.

"Yes, my lovely, we're ready."

"Quaaaaooooo." It was a snort of refreshed eagerness.

"Rhyming Cutlets indeed," said Jim, giving Doris a fond wink.

Four hours later, Neptune Bone was awoken by a gelatinous drooling into his left ear.

"Wakey, wakey, rise and whine," croaked Desdemona.

He opened his fatty eyelids quickly. As the raven-drool seeped into his ear hole, he bolted upright from where he had been lying across the two front seats. His fleshy index finger wiggled about in his ear. "Arrr, you dreadful drooling drongo. If you ever do that again I'll have your belly for a cigar case."

"Promises, promises. C'mon, chubby chops, they left hours ago."

Bone alighted from the Bugatti and plonked his fez onto his greasy hair. He took out a Belch of Brouhaha and lit it with his silver cigar-lighter. Then he stretched –

his knuckles and kneecaps cracking loudly in the quiet of the morning – and surveyed the empty ruins of Aphrodisias.

"I wish you wouldn't crack your joints like that," complained Desdemona, her eyeballs throbbing harder and redder than usual. "It gives me the collywobbles."

"There is no need for us to hurry, Desdemona. As I said, those goody-goody-aren't-we-wonderful excuses for humanity will get there and do all the finding for us."

"I just want to get outta here before that awful overblown snake comes back. I didn't sleep a wink last night ... every slither I heard had me on tentercrooks."

He blew a column of thick smoke at her. "All right, all right," he scowled – he also did not want an encounter with the Belligerent Serpent of Antiocheia. "I suppose we should get going. Besides, there's a very old Turkish bathhouse in the small village of Urgüp which I have heard good reports about. I shall stop there for an hour or so and have my tired limbs massaged and refreshed."

"Some lucky masseur will think all his birthdays have come at once when *you* walk in," Desdemona muttered sarcastically.

Bone squeezed himself back into the car. "Come, bird, the road to immortality stretches ever-beckoningly before us."

He started the car, reversed it smoothly, and, with the morning sunlight streaming around them, they motored out of Aphrodisias and onto the road heading east. "And I would appreciate it if you would perch downwind of me as we travel. You still smell like a concoction that even a baboon would reject."

"Crark. Are we nearly there yet?"

Brenda the Wonder Camel had drawn on her extra-Wonder reserves of speed and endurance that morning. So much so, that by ten o'clock – when many people had only been up and about for a few hours – she had covered nearly half the distance from Aphrodisias to Kaymaklı: almost three hundred kilometres.

"Whoa, my lovely," Jim called, slowing her down and guiding her to the shade of an enormous olive tree by the side of the road. A small stream of clear water gurgled close by. "Time for a spot of stillness for you, and as much water as you want."

"Quaaaooo." She fluttered her sweat-laden eyelashes and shook her head in a wide circle before lowering herself – first her front legs and then her rear – to the grass.

"Rark! Good pace, Bren." Doris flew up from the saddle's pommel and landed on one of the lower branches of the olive tree. She shook her wings vigorously and blinked the dust out of her eyes.

Jim climbed off the saddle and helped Meltem to do likewise. "Now I truly know why she is called a Wonder Camel," said Meltem. "All that riding, and yet I feel as if it was only three minutes ago that I climbed onto her."

"Quaaaooo," Brenda snorted modestly.

Jim unbuckled her saddle and slid it off her humps. "There, my lovely. Go and drink."

He ran his hand gently through her mane and she looked at him with her huge eyes. He gave her a wink (unseen by Meltem and Doris) and she winked back. Then she raised herself and lumbered to the edge of the stream.

Doris flew down and landed on the ground in front of Jim and Meltem, who both sat, leaning against the saddle and stretching their legs straight out in front of them. "How about some water?" asked the macaw, who had decided that there were no good claw-holds at the edge of the stream from where she could drink.

Jim took off his pith helmet and sun-spectacles and smiled. "Of course, my dear. For you, anything." He brought out his water bottle from his knapsack inside one of Brenda's saddlebags and poured a generous slurp into the lid, which also served as a cup.

Doris drank eagerly, her beak scrabbling about inside the lid and her nuggetty tongue darting in and out until the last drop had disappeared.

Without any warning, a high-pitched rendition of 'The Man I Love' blared out from somewhere close.

Doris jerked her head up and looked at Jim.

Jim looked curiously at Doris.

Doris looked at Meltem.

'The Man I Love' continued to blare.

Jim looked at Meltem.

 141

Meltem blushed and looked at Jim.

Jim raised his eyebrows and looked at Doris.

Doris opened her wings, closed them, and looked at Jim.

Jim lowered his eyebrows.

'The Man I Love' kept playing.

Then Jim and Doris both looked at Meltem and, blushing so fiercely that it seemed there were small fires burning inside her cheeks, she reached into her coat pocket and took out her mobile phone. "I changed my tune last night, before I went to sleep," she mumbled.

Jim looked at Doris and raised his eyebrows again.

Meltem flipped open the cover and the tune stopped immediately. She spoke quickly, in her business voice. "Alo! Senior Retriever of Ancientness Bottnoff speaking. *Merhaba?* Ah, hello, Mr Perry. Yes he is. I am very well, thank you. And you?" She listened for a moment, her eyes widening. "I am impressed, Mr Perry – I had no idea you were so adept on the unicycle. Would you like to speak to Jim? I'll put him on. Pardon? No, I have tied it in a bun … it is good when we are travelling to keep it under control. Yes, I prefer that too. One momentum, please. Yes, and you also."

She handed the phone to Jim and smiled. "He must have got my number from Romina at headquarters. I do hope my saxifraga is surviving."

"Hello?" said Cairo Jim into the small phone.

"Jim? Perry here. I've just learned something quite grave. Whereabouts are you?"

"Near a little country town called Hanönü Beli. We've just stopped for a breather. On our way to the underground city of Kaymaklı."

"Kaymaklı?"

Jim told Perry why they were going there, what they were seeking, and what they had already found out and discovered. During this, Doris waddled up and down next to him, contributing details she thought Perry should know, like what a wretchedly vile low-life Bone was, and how enormous and slithery the Belligerent Serpent of Antiocheia had been and how Hieronymous von Nozzel was a Barry Manilow fan. Jim relayed all this information to Perry, who started getting a bit confused after a few minutes.

"All right," the old man finally said. "It sounds like you're getting somewhere. I only rang to stress – not that you need this to be stressed, Jim, you know that cad better'n most – that Bone *must* be stopped. Absolutely and fully! Just by chance I was talking to one of our members here at the Society – a woman who spent her entire career studying the cult of Artemis – and she told me, a few moments ago, that if any of Artemis' sacred relics are to be reactivated again, then this could, within all the bounds of probability, herald the very end of nature itself!"

"The very end of nature?" Jim's blood began to chill.

"Exactly. Forget about the seasons as we know 'em now. Whoever can dredge up the ancient powers of the Great Goddess, *through invoking a combination of her Sacred Objects*, can control and change the course of all that has been! From what you've just told me about this Petticoat and the Buckle of Abundance and the Belt of Bountaiety and the Barry Manilow records, it sounds like Bone is hurtling towards that possibility. Though I don't know what Barry Manilow has to do with it..."

Jim's forehead was quickly dotting with beads of fresh perspiration.

"I'd better go," Perry said, "and let you all get on with it. Bone and that ratbag of a raven are probably creeping through Kaymaklı as we speak. Don't let 'em get that Belt, Jim. And guard the Buckle with your life, if you'll excuse my melodramatic insistence. But I'm an old man, and I'm allowed such indulgences."

"Don't worry," said the archaeologist-poet, patting the Buckle inside his shirt pocket and trying to sound confident, "it's safe with us."

Perry's voice lowered to a near-whisper. "Don't tell Meltem, but I've introduced a new burger into m' take-away pigeon restaurants. 'The Meltem Moment' I call it, a pigeon burger so succulent that it melts in your mouth. Ooer, must go – Sturgeon Lombeck has got his head stuck in a saucepan from the Fifth Dynasty. Stupid man, I told him there was nothing to see that far inside the thing. Best of luck, Jim! Cheerio!"

"Goodbye, Perry," replied Jim, but the line had already dropped out.

"Rerk! What did he have to say?"

The urgency of the job at hand had come rushing back into every fibre of Jim's being. He stood and put his pith helmet and sun-spectacles back on. "We have to leave now," he said. "This is even more serious than we've dared let ourselves think!"

16

SOME SUDDEN INTRUSIONS

WITH HER HOOFS POWERED by an extra-zestful burst of exuberance, Brenda the Wonder Camel transported Cairo Jim, Doris and Meltem Bottnoff eastwards into the region known as Cappadocia.

At first they travelled through a wide, open landscape with green fields and farms all around. Off in the distance to the north, great mountains were distantly visible, their pinnacles white against the bright blue crispness of the sky.

Brenda maintained her pace the whole way, never once faltering or losing her concentration. Meltem gripped Jim's waist and let herself sway with Brenda's ongoing motion: on and ahead, on and ahead, *clopta-clopta-clopta-clop*.

Doris perched steadfastly on the forward pommel of the saddle, her small eyes keeping watch on the road ahead. Occasionally a large, overloaded truck would appear in the gentle haze ahead and, as it approached, Doris would bend low and warn Brenda of its approach. The Wonder Camel could see the truck long before Doris could, but Brenda was never going to let her small feathered friend know this telepathically: it made Doris feel slightly important

during the journey, and Brenda respected this.

Jim of Cairo stared grimly ahead, his mind filled with the prospect of Bone reactivating some long-forgotten and dormant power that would ultimately bode no good for the world. Even though Bone had been a constant enemy and threat to the peace of their world for many years now, Jim could never get used to the idea that such malevolence existed. It was as though each time Bone hatched some devious, threatening scheme, it was the first time that Cairo Jim had had to deal with it.

As Brenda galloped along, and as the scenery passed by in what was a constant blur of colour and smells, the rhythm of Brenda's movement fused with the poetry cells in Jim's brain, and a verse lit up in his mind. He didn't speak it aloud, but it stayed in his head for much of the journey:

> There are pockets of our History
> best left undisturbed –
> great mysteries and knowledge
> not meant to be perturbed.
> What happens when we obtrude
> with what has been forgot?
> We tamper with the fragile mood
> of History's melting pot.

Try as he might, he couldn't get the foreboding verse out of his system.

After nearly three hours, the scenery changed dramatically.

What had been horizon-stretching green fields bordered by majestic mountains now gave way to a panorama that might have been from another planet. The flatness of the land became a series of tall, conical pinnacles. Sheer towers of rock rose up and away for farther than the eye could see.

Atop many of these pointed towers, there were balanced – as if by a miracle of nature – enormous, round boulders of harder rock. It seemed as though all it would take to unbalance the boulders, and send them toppling and crashing to the ground so far below, would be a gentle breeze or the honking of a car horn.

Jim pulled gently on the reins. "Whoa, my lovely."

"Quaoooo." Brenda slowed to a halt, the sweat running down her mane and dripping from her eyebrows.

"Cappadocia," said Meltem, loosening her grip on Jim's waist. "The famous Fairy Chimneys."

"Raaark!" Doris moved her body quickly up and down, and stretched her wings wide. "'This is the fairy land'," she quoted from *The Comedy of Errors*, Act Two, Scene Two, by William Shakespeare.

"Swoggle me softly in stone," whispered Jim. He took off his sun-spectacles. "Look. There are doorways and little windows in the chimneys. Dotted all over the place!"

Brenda cast her eyes over the beautiful formations. To her they looked strong yet frail at the same time.

"Meltem?"

"Yes, Doris?"

"Fairies don't *really* live in them, do they?" (The macaw didn't believe in fairies and the like, but this was not her country, and she was respectful of the fact that things might be different in Turkey.)

Jim did a small swivel and looked at Meltem, waiting for her answer.

Meltem smiled as she looked into his bright blue eyes before answering Doris. "No, no, there are no fairies here. These towers were called Fairy Chimneys long ago, because people thought that they'd be the kinds of houses fairies would live in if they had houses. No, these chimneys were all made by the wind."

"The wind," repeated Jim, taking in the towers once again.

"Most of the rock," Meltem said, "that you see out there is very soft. It is volcanic tuff, some of the softest rock on all of the planet. The wind is extremely strong in these valleys at times, and it whips around the rock, eroding it and wearing it down. The wind, sand and rain have made the tapered shapes you see, and a rock of harder material is often left perched precariously on the tops of many of the towers."

Jim let out an impressed whistle. "Who lived in all the towers?"

"The local people, until modern times, when they were moved elsewhere. For perhaps 2000 years people

carved rooms in them, high up, as you can see. And then they carved dwellings underground, for protection from invaders."

The word *protection* shot down Jim's spine, like an ice cube slipping down his shirt. There was a lot that needed protection right now. "We should go," he said, replacing his sun-spectacles. "How far to Kaymaklı, Meltem?"

"Not far. Not now."

"Rark, let's move!"

"Let's get that Belt and see if we can get Bone at the same time!"

"Quaooo," snorted Brenda as Jim nudged her into motion once more.

Neptune Flannelbottom Bone was lying on his over-bloated stomach on an old massage bench in the 400-year-old Ürgüp Delight Turkish Bath and Steam House. He was completely naked, except for a threadbare yellow towel which barely covered his lower region.

"Crark!" grunted Desdemona, sitting on a shelf on the opposite wall and doing her best to cope with the copious amounts of steam that seeped into the room. "Where is that big guy with the moustache? I wanna get outta here... I can feel my fleas boiling, and they don't like that. Ouch!"

"At least the steam is lessening your sickening smelliness. The man with the moustache will be here in a few momentums, you impatient insignia of ingratitude. He will come in and give me my massage, after which we can motor back to Kaymaklı and finish off that virtuous brigade of do-gooders. But not before relieving them of the Belt of Bountaiety and the Buckle, of course."

"I don't know why I bother hanging round with you. I'd be better off being a slug."

Bone ashed his cigar on the floor. "Why wish for that which you already are?"

"Very funny. Ha-crark-ha!"

The drive had been a good, smooth one – a Bugatti, as Bone knew, never delivers less, and now, as he lay there with the perspiration oozing out of his countless adipose pores, forming pools of prune-smelling sweat on the bench and floor beneath him, Bone was feeling very smug and almost relaxed. So much so, that he started to sing – in a rumbling baritone – a song of anticipation:

"Soon the whole world order will be mine
   – mine to bend and distort.
Soon the summer sunlight will turn to winter's rime
   – who would have ever thought? Arrrr.

"Soon I'll alter seasons, making brightness dim
   – I shall turn it around.
I'll wallop all the weather; I'll bend it to my whim
   – the barren shall become fruitful ground. Arrrr.

 151

I shall be the Ruler, Father Nature to the world!
Rainy night becomes sunny day!
The Greenhouse Effect's History, its memory
torn and curled,
The legacy of Artemis shall roll my flag unfurled,
I'll own all gold and diamonds, every oyster
that is pearled,
THANKS TO LEGENDARY LINGERIE. ARRRR!"

"Oh, for the love of Caruso! Nevermore, nevermore, nevermore!"

"You're jealous," Bone sneered. "Just because every time you open your beak it sounds like you're gargling with sandpaper in your throat."

"At least I don't look like a subcontinent when I lie down."

"Enshut your beak, Desdemona, lest I permanently enshut it with a bolt of lightning when I have all of Artemis' powers."

She kept quiet, looking at him with her slitted, throbbing eyeballs.

"You know something?" he said, puffing grandiosely on his cigar. "I've just had a thought."

"I hope it didn't get lonely in that head of yours," she muttered to herself.

"It seems to me," Bone said, oblivious to her muttering, "that it would be a great waste to destroy Cairo Jim and his cohorts as soon as he has discovered the final pieces to our archaeological jigsaw puzzle. No, that would be a dreadful thing."

"Eh?"

"Don't you think it would be altogether better for us if we were to wait a tad longer? If, as soon as Jim and the goody brigade have found the Belt, we were to *capture* them, confiscate the Belt and the Buckle, and then take them with us, to the place from where I have decided to unleash my new powers?"

"You mean, force Jim and that gaudy Doris and the camel and the woman with 'em to *watch* what you can do?"

"That's exactly what I mean. Force them to watch me. Arrr. It will drive them positively nuts, to finally see the power which for so long I have deserved, and which will be once and indisputably for ever, MINE!"

"To *finally* see?"

"To finally see. Because, after they have witnessed the power that was once the power of Artemis and which is now the power of Bone, they shall *see no more*. Arrrrrrr!"

"Crark crark crark. That's rubbing it in!" Desdemona's eyes throbbed demonically at the thought.

Just then the big man with the moustache came in, carrying a large bottle of oil and a dozen towels. "I'LL SHOW YOU WHAT RUBBING IN IS," boomed the man enthusiastically.

"Sh," hissed Bone to the raven, "not another word now. I am about to have my—*ooooffff!*"

The big man had flipped Bone roughly over and was kneading his upper chest with his brawny, hairy hands.

"Arrr, steady on, big boy. You'll break something if you—*eeeerrrrrrffffff!*"

The man smiled, showing several gaps in his teeth.

"Go for it, daddy-oh," croaked Desdemona.

The man poured half the bottle of oil over Bone, and slid him fiercely along the bench so that Bone's fez crumpled against the wall.

"*Oooorrrrggghhhh!* Careful, you King Kong impersonator! *Gnnnkk!* Mind my tassel! *Oh! Oooocchhhh!*"

With mighty slaps and much clenching and pinching of Bone's hide, the man with the moustache started working the fleshy expanse, pummelling the wobbling skin as though it were tough jelly.

"Lighter, lighter, please—*ooooffff*—I am a tender—*oowwwwwwwcccchhh!* I bruise easily, and—*Aaaarrrggghhhh! Ow!* No, not there—*yaaaarrrrrlllll! Ooofff! Eeerrrrrffff!* Have mercy—*oooooffffff! Heeeeerrrrrrgggghhh! Oooffff* – ooh, haven't we met somewhere before? *Ooofff! Yowwwwwww! Gggnnnkkkk!* Look, I think I've changed my—*Aaaawwwwggghhh! Yowwwccchhh!* No, don't go down there—*whoooooooo!* I barely know you, sir! *Whooh whooh whooh whooh!*"

And so Bone spent the next two hours in the steamy pleasure of an old Turkish custom, while Desdemona enjoyed herself more than she had enjoyed herself for ages.

17

...CITY OF KAYMAKLı

"THERE IT IS," said Meltem, taking her hand from Jim's waist and pointing straight ahead. "The underground city of Kaymaklı."

"Whoa, my lovely!" Jim brought the Wonder Camel to a gradual halt by a low, wide mound of earth with long, thick grass growing on the top.

Doris flexed herself up and down on the pommel. "Rark. Looks like some old hill."

Brenda lowered herself to the ground, her nostrils flaring as she breathed in the still air. Quickly Jim alighted and helped Meltem from the saddle.

"It does indeed," said Meltem, shaking the dust from her hair. "But look carefully, there, over to the left. See? There is a small opening."

"There it is," said Jim, getting a water bottle and pan from Brenda's saddlebag. He poured a big slosh into the pan and she drank it eagerly.

"Quaooo!"

"A doorway," Doris squawked.

When Brenda had finished drinking, the four of them went to the heavy wooden door. It was bolted and padlocked shut.

"How do we get in?" said Doris.

Meltem smiled and reached into her pocket. "Leave that to me." She took out a long, thin key with the word 'WHOOPSADAISIE' engraved along the edge.

"My job has a lot of special privileges, one of which is my WHOOPSADAISIE."

"Your what?" said Cairo Jim.

"My Worldwide Hindrance Obliterator, Old Prevention Smasher, Archaeological Deterrent Annihilator In Serious Investigative Emergencies."

"Of course," blinked Doris.

Meltem slid her WHOOPSADAISIE into the lock. "This key fits every lock, keyhole, clasp, fastener and latch at any archaeological site around the world. Watch." With a sharp turn of her wrist, the lock clicked loudly, and Meltem pushed the door open. "Come," she said, entering the opening.

"I should get our torches ready," Jim muttered.

"No need," Meltem said. Jim, Doris and Brenda followed her into the dimness and found themselves in a space the size of a small room. Meltem went to a big metal box attached to the opposite wall of rock.

She inserted her WHOOPSADAISIE once again, this time into a tiny hole on the door of the box. Another click, and she opened the door. Inside was a row of electric light switches.

"The underground city has been equipped with light so that the many tourists who come through here do not fall and break their necks." She flicked all the switches down, and a weak, yellowy light glowed above them.

"Luckily for us Kaymaklı is at the moment closed to all tourists, while restoration is being carried out."

"So the restorers will be down here with us?" Jim asked.

"No." Meltem closed the door of the box and locked it again. "They are on strike at the moment. They are demanding brushes with softer bristles and contoured handles, and the government is not buckling to their outrageous demands."

"Hmm," hmmed Doris.

Brenda peered into the opening that led out of the room and further down into the underground. Everything ahead – the corridors she could see weaving away at all angles; the thin, spindly columns; the well-worn, sloping steps and the small alcoves – was of the same colour: the colour of the rock. A light, speckly brown. Lit by the weak, yellowy light bulbs that hung down like carnival lights, the whole place looked very dry and dusty.

"We should stay together," Meltem said quietly. "There are many passages in this city, and tourists get lost regularly. Our archaeologists are always finding new rooms in here or undiscovered stairways. And sometimes tourists who were lost for *too long*."

"Let's go then," Jim said. He removed his sun-spectacles, put them in his pocket, and then stopped. "One thing first, though. Brenda, may I?"

"Quaoooo."

He delved into one of her saddlebags and, after some

 157

searching, brought out a large ball of string. "The Old Relics Society's motto," he told Meltem, "is 'You Never Know When You'll Need a Good Bit of String'. No better time than now, I reckon."

"Rark! Good thinking. Can I be the unraveller?"

"Of course, my dear." He gave Doris the string, and the feathers round the edge of her beak crinkled happily. "If you don't mind going last."

"Nope," she said. "Not if we stay together I don't." She briskly wound the end of the string around a large rock.

"Keep your eyes open for any signs of egg motifs," Jim said to them all. "Chances are, Caius Vibius Salutaris used the decoration here as well, as a clue to where the Belt is."

And so off they set, into the first passage.

"The Hittite people made this city," Meltem said as they went along, "to hide and to live whenever there was an invasion by warring neighbours. As many as 10,000 people lived here in Kaymaklı, it is believed."

"Coo," cooed Doris, hop-fluttering at the rear and slowly unravelling the string behind her to leave a trail back to the first room.

They went down some stairs, deeper into the ground. To the left and right they came across countless other doorways, all of them small (Brenda would have had to crouch very low if she had wanted to pass through them). Some of these doorways led off to other passages which disappeared around corners or further downwards at dangerous-looking angles. Other doorways led into tiny rooms or large, cavernous spaces.

Then Jim stopped and let out a whistle. "Swoggle me circularly," he gasped.

"Quaooo!" snorted Brenda.

They had halted before a gigantic stone disc, perfectly round and about half a metre thick. It was standing on its side, the top of it leaning up against a wall. In the centre of the disc was a small round hole, big enough for Jim to pass his arm through up to his elbow.

"A mobile doorway," Meltem said. "Be careful, Jim, don't get your arm caught in there." Gently she helped him withdraw his arm, her fingers brushing against his wrist for a little too long, Doris thought.

"*Reeeerraarrk!* A mobile door?"

Meltem jumped, and put her hand on her heart. "Yes, Doris. We'll see a few of these in here. The Hittites made them so that if the enemies outside found their way inside, the Hittites could roll the door down this channel" – she indicated a wide groove gouged into the floor, and sloping down towards them – "to seal themselves off from the enemies."

"Ingenious," Jim murmured, running his hands over the disc. "C'mon, let's keep going. Don't forget about that string, my dear."

"Of course not," Doris prerked. "When there's a job to do, I do it."

Down they trudged, passing rooms lined with ancient stone urns and pots. "Storage jars," said Jim, his skin tingling with the sight of ancient civilisation's orderliness.

"They used them for water and grain and wine and oils," said Meltem. "Come into this room for a moment," she beckoned. Jim, Brenda and Doris followed her, Brenda stooping low to get through the doorway.

For a few moments they stood still and silent. Then Meltem whispered. "I can hear it now."

"Rerk. Hear what? All I can hear is my heart beating under my plumage."

"Quaaaooo," snorted Brenda. *It's a stream!*"

Jim picked up on her thought a split second before he heard the sound. "It's a stream," he blurted.

"An underground stream," smiled Meltem. "See through that hole there? Be careful – it's a long drop."

They peered through the opening in the floor at the end of the storage room. Far, far below, a dark surface glistened and rippled.

"One of many deep pools made by the Hittites," Meltem told them. "This is how they were able to survive for so long down here. Sometimes they remained here for over a year without venturing up to the ground. They were even able to use the water to grow vegetables."

"What a race," Jim whispered, and his whisper echoed against the walls of the well.

"A race, a race, a race..."

"This chattering won't buy pussy a new bonnet," Doris said. "Remember, Bone's out there somewhere!"

"What a disgrace," Jim said loudly, and the echo came again:

"Disgrace, disgrace, disgrace..."

Onwards they crept, down passageways and up staircases, through cavernous entrances and small apertures carved into the rock. With every step and hop-flutter they took, they kept their eyes wide open for any signs of egg decorations.

At one stage, Brenda poked her head into a chamber that opened off from the right side of the passageway they were in. She sniffed the air. There was something different about this chamber; something that smelled sweeter than the others.

Curious, she pushed her neck in and looked around. Then her humps followed her neck, and then her back legs, until – without realising it – the Wonder Camel had entered the chamber completely, and was walking slowly through it.

(Doris had been unaware of Brenda's disappearance ... the macaw had been concentrating intently on unravelling the ball of string while at the same time looking out for the egg motifs. Thus engaged, she had waddled beneath Brenda, through her legs and under her body, and was in front of her when Brenda had entered the chamber.)

Inside the chamber, Brenda turned to the left. Here, a smaller corridor rose upwards, sloping gently. Carefully she clip-clopped along. With a quiet flick of her mane, she kept going through the corridor, further and further, intrigued by the uncertainty.

On the other side of the wall, Jim turned to check on Doris and Brenda. "Brenda?" he said when he saw the empty space where she should have been.

Doris stopped unravelling and also turned. "Rark! That's strange. It sounded like she was right behind me!"

"Listen," whispered Meltem.

The clip-clop-clip-clop of Brenda's hoofs came, loudly and clearly.

"Sounds like she's right with us," Jim said. He took off his pith helmet and scratched his head. "But she's not."

Meltem knocked on the wall of rock. "I think she's on the other side of this. That's one other strange thing about these underground cities – sound carries brilliantly. Sometimes you can hear other people who are in rooms hundreds of metres away, and they sound as if they are standing right next to you, speaking in their normal voices without shouting or anything."

"Brenda," Jim said, not raising his voice. "Can you hear me?"

"Quaaaooo," came a clear snort from the other side of the wall.

"Rerk, where are you, Bren?"

"Quaooo."

There was more clip-clopping and then, in a small window-hole above Jim's head, Brenda's front hoofs appeared.

"My lovely!" Jim said. "Come back and join us, before we get horribly separated."

Her hoofs moved forward along the corridor, and

Jim, Doris and Meltem saw her back hoofs going past. Then these disappeared from sight. After a few anxious moments of clip-clopping, they heard her give a louder snort.

And there she was, in front of them, emerging through a small doorway.

Jim rubbed her snout. "Now stay with us, you lovely creature. Don't go wandering again. The last thing we need is to lose you."

She snorted, blinked her lashes, and turned to lead the way down the passage.

"How nice and courteous of them. They've turned on all the lights for us. Arrrr."

"C'mon, bruisy-boy, let's go get 'em and that Belt!"

"Shhh. Listen, you perfumed parcel of putridity. I can hear them talking."

Desdemona cocked her head and heard the snatch of conversation drifting along through the underground world:

"...stay with us, you lovely creature. Don't go wandering again. The last thing we need is to lose you."

"That's Jim, all right," she croaked. "All sweetness and lovey-dovey-durdah. Blecchhh!"

"And see, they've left a trail of string! This is going to be easier than we thought. Come on, stay close to me. And be careful with that Splatto Miniature Cannon. We might not need it, but I want it in perfect working order if we *do*."

BREAKING OF THE EGGS

FIFTEEN MINUTES LATER, Brenda, Jim, Meltem and Doris came to another huge stone disc leaning against the wall.

"Another mobile door," said Jim. "Much bigger than the other one. Thicker, too."

"Look," Doris pointed with her wing. "The passage descends."

"Quaooo," Brenda snorted, leading them onwards and downwards. The passage was only just wide enough for her to fit through.

They continued, inspecting every part of the walls around them, searching into each small niche and peering into all the cubicles that led from the passage.

Doris, concentrating intently on her string and on her looking, suddenly gave a small squawk and stopped. The others kept going.

The macaw lowered the ball of string to the ground, and squinted at the wall beside her. Slowly she waddled closer to it, her claws trembling with hope and anticipation. *Had she really seen what she thought she had seen?*

Now her beak was almost touching the wall, and she could feel the dust that caked it – dust that had not been

cleared for centuries and centuries. She narrowed her eyes and concentrated hard.

Yes! It was!

She stepped back and looked higher up the wall. Raising her wings, she rose into the air. Then she hovered, still and scrutinising.

Here was another, the same as the first!

She fluttered to the left, and up a bit. Another one, almost smothered in dust, but the faint outline unmistakable: a small, simple egg-shape, carved into the rock.

"Reeeeeerrrrrraaaaaaaaaaaarrrrrkkkkk!" she screeched. "Bingo, whacko, spotto the diddlio!"

Jim, Meltem and Brenda came rushing back to see what the fuss was all about.

"Look," Doris squawked proudly. "Look carefully. All over the wall here, the pattern!"

The other three narrowed their eyes and stared. Gradually, as they stopped seeing just a flat surface caked with dust, they too discerned the small patterns.

"Swoggle me subtly," Jim gasped. "Doris, you've found the first clue!"

"One of Artemis' fertility symbols," whispered Meltem, her eyes filling with the sight of the hundreds of faint eggs decorating the wall.

"Quaaooo," thought Brenda. *"The wall is a different colour to everywhere else. Slightly paler."*

Jim caught her observation, almost as soon as she had thought it. "Well look at this. The wall's a different

colour to everywhere else. Slightly paler. Even through all this dust you can still tell." He raised his fist and gave a soft knock on the surface.

Boomp!

With his fist still raised, he went to the opposite wall and knocked on that.

Boonk!

He came back to the dusty egg wall and knocked again.

Boomp!

"Rerk! It's hollow!"

"I'd say it's plaster," said Jim. "And I'd say it's hiding something." He reached into one of Brenda's saddle-bags and pulled out his small Expose All! Combination Pick, Sledgehammer and Letter-opener.

"Very clever of Salutaris," whispered Meltem, watching Jim as he rolled his sleeves a bit higher.

"Stand back, everyone, and beware of flying plaster. I don't want to destroy this wall, just make an opening big enough for us to see what's on the other side. But there will be a bit of mess."

"Quaooo." Brenda moved round in front of Meltem, and brought her back against the opposite wall.

Doris flew up and nestled between Brenda's humps. "You be careful yourself, Jim."

"I will, my dear. Here goes."

He raised the hammer part of the implement and brought it hard against the wall.

Crack!

And again.

Craaaccckkk!

Six strong blows later, and a thick cloud of dusty powder was rising from the fallen plaster on the ground. More plaster fell than Jim had anticipated; the opening in the wall was large enough for them all to pass though.

"It'll be dark," Doris cooed, poking her beak and a wing into a saddlebag. "We'll need the torches."

"Only one torch," said Jim. "Doesn't look very deep in there."

Doris flew to him with his torch in her beak.

"Thank you, my dear."

"You're welcome."

He turned it on and shone the beam into the opening. "It's just an alcove, with a..." His voice trailed off.

"With a what?" Doris asked, twitching by his boots.

"What, Jim?" Meltem came closer. "What can you see?"

"Quaaooo? Quaaooo?"

Every pore of Cairo Jim's skin was tingling as if a mild voltage of electrical current had entered his body. The hairs behind his kneecaps stood on end, and his eyebrows bristled with a discoverer's extreme delight.

"Look for yourselves," he said, his voice barely audible.

He moved slightly to one side. Doris fluttered up onto his shoulder, and Meltem came closer. Brenda, at the back, stripped away the gloom in the alcove with her powerful Wonder Camel vision.

For a few moments there was complete silence as the four of them beheld what was in the alcove. The quietness was so overwhelming that Jim could hear his heart beating the rhythm of a fierce tango.

Then Meltem uttered the name. "Artemis."

There, set back in the tiny alcove, the ancient Goddess smiled at them. She was carved onto the wall, so that Her image was not free-standing, but appeared to be breaking out of the rock behind Her. Like the great statue back at the museum in Istanbul, this Artemis was adorned with many full fruits, eggs and pomegranates and aubergines, carved and hanging from Her stone Petticoat, and Her crown was identical: rising tiers of three small temples supported by the griffins and sphinxes.

Unlike the Artemis at Istanbul, this Artemis was small: no bigger than half a metre.

Jim moved the torchbeam down the figure, slowly over Her Petticoat. "Look, there's a Belt of Bountaiety carved onto Her waist. What're those letters... C, V, S?"

"Caius Vibius Salutaris," Doris cooed. "This is what he made!"

"Quaaooo," Brenda snorted, having glimpsed something below in the spill of the torchbeam.

"Look," Meltem gasped. "On that shelf underneath Her!"

As the shelf of rock lit up fully, Jim's mouth sprang into a wide smile, and his eyes pricked with the overwhelming excitement that doesn't come to a

person very often in the one day. He gulped and felt his hands trembling.

"I think we've found it," he muttered happily.

There, resting on the shelf, folded neatly like a sleeping snake, was a dazzling belt of wide gold panels. Each panel was adorned with an intricately fashioned silver egg, each egg as perfect as the first egg ever created.

"The Belt of Bountaiety," Jim whispered, reaching in and carefully removing it from the shelf of rock. "We've found it, and the Buckle. Everything has come together."

"Arrr. Listen. They've got it!"

"Drat 'em," throbbed Desdemona.

"We will, we will, just get a move on with that wooden pole!"

"Why do I hafta do all the sweaty work?"

"Shut up and lever!"

"Rark! This belt does 'dazzle mine eyes, or do I see three suns?' As Shakespeare wrote in *Henry VI, Part Three*, Act Two, Scene One."

"It is gorgeous," Meltem said. "You are right, Doris – there is such brightness there that it could be coming from the heavens."

"Those ancient goldsmiths," sighed Jim, turning the Belt over in his hands. "Such a work of beauty."

Then Brenda heard something. "Quaaooo," she snorted quietly.

"What, Bren?" Doris hop-fluttered from Jim's shoulder to the top of his pith helmet. "What's wrong?"

The Wonder Camel was still and silent, her head raised and her nostrils twitching. Her ears stood straight up, attentive and alert.

The sound came again. A low, soft rumble, like thunder from far away.

Bbbbbbrrrrrrrrrrrrrrrrr.

"Quaaaoooo!"

"She can hear something," Doris squawked, "and she doesn't like it, whatever it is!"

The rumbling was increasing, and seemed to be coming closer.

BBBBBBBbbbbrrrrrrrrrrrrrrrrrrrrrrrrrrrrrrrr.

Now it was loud enough for them all to feel the vibrations as the noise shuddered towards them.

BBBBBBBBBBBBBBBBBBrrrrrrrrrrrrrrrrrrrrrrrrrrrrrrrrrrrr-rrrr!

"It's another earthquake!" Meltem shouted.

"No," Brenda thought, *"it's something rolling down a passage nearby!"*

"Screeeeeeeerrrkkkk!" Doris screeched. "It's not an earthquake, it's something rolling down a passage nearby!"

The rumbling was louder by the second – it was vibrating against the rock walls and the floor and against the ribcages of Jim, Doris, Meltem and Brenda.

Suddenly, far up the sloping floor, Brenda saw it. "Quaaaoooo!"

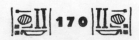

Jim, Doris and Meltem saw it too. "The mobile door!" yelled Jim. "It's rolling down *this* passage, and towards us!"

The enormous disc of rock was rolling slowly but steadily down along the groove in the floor. Its tread was so thick it completely filled the passageway, its curved edges bumping against the passage walls as it moved forward. A great, groaning grinding blasted from beneath it as it rolled along the groove.

BBBBRRRRR-RRRRRR-RRRRRRRR-RRR-RRR-RRRRRRRRRRRRRRRRRR!

Jim spun around the other way to try and find a means of escape. "No!" he shouted – nothing but a dead-end wall. There were no doorways in front; the only doors were back up the passage, and, second by second, the rolling disc was moving past those doors, closer and closer to Brenda, Jim, Doris and Meltem.

Grit and dust billowed out from beneath the disc, filling the passage with a thick mist.

"Jim!" Doris screeched. "Where can we go?" They couldn't get past the disc, to where the doorways were; not even an ant could have cleared the space between disc and walls.

"It's gaining speed," cried Meltem as the noise grew louder and the disc started rolling faster and faster.

Brenda threw her mane back and snorted a shrill, urgent directive: *"Quick, all of you, press yourselves into the alcove as much as you can. Flatten yourselves in there – I'll see what I can do!"*

Jim grasped her thought and pulled Meltem into the small recess of the alcove with him, making sure Doris was still on his pith helmet. "Hurry! Up against the opening here! Breathe in, Meltem, as much as you can! Brenda! Brenda, my lovely, come in – we'll make extra room! Hurry, or the disc will—"

"*QUUUAAAAOOOOOO!*" She shook her head, snorted the dust from her nostrils, and took a deep breath. The Wonder Camel had made a decision. She had sized up the situation, and realised that there was no way she, or her friends, could fully stop the disc. There was not enough time for that.

But she could *delay* it. She could slow down its course until it got to the Artemis alcove. Then she could bundle herself sideways into the alcove, having slowed the disc a bit, and let the disc continue. This way, the impact of the disc when it hit the wall below would be lessened, and there would be less chance of the wall – and maybe the entire city of Kaymaklı – collapsing from the collision. And once the disc had rolled past the alcove, Jim, Doris, Meltem and Brenda could emerge and retreat up the passageway, through one of the doorways.

She squinted through the gritty, dusty cloud, and heard the near-deafening rumble. Through the wafting debris she caught sight of the disc: it was about four metres away, and rolling towards her.

"Brenda, come in here! Get out of its way! You'll be—"

"*QUAAAAAAAAAAOOOOOOOOOO!*" Don't stand

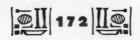

still against it, she told herself. If it hits you at that speed it will be bad. No, run and face it. Rush at it and counteract the force!

This she decided to do.

The noble Wonder Camel lowered her neck and head until they were close to the floor. Then, like a tightly coiled spring, she let herself go, charging past the alcove and up the sloping floor.

Just as she was about to make contact with the disc, she turned herself slightly to the side, so that her humps – her strongest parts, and the most cushioned – would take the full impact.

There was a sudden *oooooofffff* as her back hit the tread. Brenda gasped at the huge weight against her. For a second, the rolling slowed as she pushed ever harder. Hard against, hard against, hard against!

Then, as Brenda knew it would, her slowing of the disc reached its maximum point. The disc had slowed as much as it would. As gravity set in, the colossal weight of the stone began to regain its full inertia. With rapid momentum it kept rolling, pushing Brenda down the slope, closer and closer to the dead-end wall at the bottom.

"No!" cried Jim, watching through the settling dust. "Brenda, no!"

On rolled the disc, and backwards stepped Brenda. On and backwards, on and backwards, on and backwards. With each slip of rotation, the disc was pulling at her hairs – scrunching them downwards towards the ground. Brenda had to move infinitesimally away from the disc and then back onto it, over and over, to avoid slipping under its path.

The sweat poured from her body, making the floor slipperier and slipperier.

Brenda could see the alcove approaching as she was being pushed downwards. Another two seconds, she calculated, and she would have to bundle herself in there.

But, just as she reached the spot where she had to leave the disc, her hoofs slipped in the sweat-filled groove below. The disc came down harder, and the Wonder Camel lost her footing.

Scrabbling wildly, her hoofs shot out in all directions. With a quick sliding, she found her balance, and regained her stance, still pushing against the force.

"Bren!" screeched Doris. "Step in here! Come in here now!"

But the disc had pushed her past the Artemis alcove, and Brenda had lost her chance to join her friends.

Jim, Doris and Meltem watched aghast as Brenda and the disc passed. The rough edges of the stone came within millimetres of their noses and beak.

When the disc had gone by, Doris, Jim and Meltem leapt out of the alcove. Now they couldn't see Brenda on the other side of the disc – every bit of the passage-way was filled with the rolling disc. Jim ran after it and tried to pull it backwards, towards him, to slow it. But his attempt failed – the surface of the tread was too smooth for him to get a grip, and he kept sliding down the tread.

"*QUUAAAAAOOOOOO!*" came Brenda's distressed snort from the other side, as the disc began to wedge her against the wall.

"My lovely!" Jim hollered. "My lovely!"

"*REEEEEEEEEEEEAAAAAAAARRRRRRKKKK!*" Doris cried, a great lamentation of grief ripping out from her beak.

Then, in the blink of an eye, the disc gave a huge shudder and ground to a halt.

And there was quiet – dusty, sweaty, panic-laced quiet.

"Brenda," called Jim. "Snort something!"

No answer.

"Bren," crowed Doris. "Tell us you're there?"

A faint sound emerged from the other side of the disc: a scrabbling of hoofs and a quiet, scared snorting.

"She's alive," said Meltem.

"*Jim,*" Brenda implored telepathically. "*I'm stuck. Pinned against the wall by this weight.*"

"She's stuck," Jim said, terror filling his voice. "I can feel it in my bones. She's pinned against the wall by this weight."

"We have to get her out," said Doris.

"Yes." Meltem nodded. She squatted down and inspected the groove in the floor. "This region is on one of the major earthquake fault lines in Turkey." She whispered so that Brenda would not hear her. "All it would take would be a little tremor to set the disc off again. It's just a matter of time before there's another tremor, or worse, and then the disc would—"

She left her sentence unfinished and rose.

"Make Wonder Camel pâté, perhaps?" came a snarl from above.

Jim, Doris and Meltem spun around. There, further up the passageway, stood Neptune Bone, his legs apart and his pudgy fists on his pudgier hips, looking like an over-inflated Colossus.

On the ground, between his legs, Desdemona gloated down at them. Strapped to the top of her skull was the Splatto Miniature Cannon, and it was aimed directly at the head of Cairo Jim.

19

BETWEEN A ROCK
AND A HARD PLACE

THE LIGHT WAS GOING CRAZY.

When the disc had rolled down the passageway, it had bumped against the electrical light globes strung across the passage ceiling. Some of the globes had shattered, but those that had not were now swinging back and forth, casting wild, dizzy shadows across the walls and all that was in the passageway.

"Arrr," snarled Bone, his beard bristling with great delight. "Don't make a move, Jim. Even so much as a flicker of your nostril hairs, and Desdemona will send a miniature cannonball straight through your forehead."

"And it'll blow *you* to smithereens as well," Desdemona croaked at Doris, still perched atop Jim's pith helmet.

"Rark! You fleabag, you gunkbucketed—"

"Enshut your beak!" exclaimed the raven.

"Keep that cannon fixed firmly on them," Bone ordered Desdemona as he made his way carefully down the slope. After a few moments, and puffing heavily, he came face to face with Cairo Jim.

"I'll have that, thank you very much!" Bone grabbed the gold and silver Belt of Bountaiety from Jim's hands.

"Take it," Jim said. "Take it, but leave us! Brenda's

trapped on the other side of this disc, and if we don't do something soon, she'll not survive!"

"Shut up, Mr Goodyboy. I have a little searching to do."

His fat hands padded across Jim's shirt. "Arrr, what have we in here?"

Doris opened her wings and closed them again.

"Keep 'em still, dolly-bird," rasped Desdemona.

With a savage yank, Bone ripped Jim's pocket clear from his shirt and caught the Buckle of Abundance before it dropped to the floor.

"Just what we need," he sneered, turning the Buckle over in his hands. The swinging lights made the sacred object glint brightly.

He put it into his waistcoat pocket and turned to Meltem. "I do not think, madam, that you have had the pleasure of making my esteemed acquaintance. I am Captain Neptune Flannelbottom Bone, one of the world's most pre-eminent archaeologists and acquisitors of fine arts. And you are?"

"Very unhappy to meet you," answered Meltem, thrusting out her petite chin defiantly.

Bone's eyes flashed momentarily. "Feisty, aren't we? Never mind, I don't think you're in a position to be a great threat to me and my plan of the total domination of every force of nature known to humankind. Spread your arms, madam, for you also must be searched."

Still with her chin out-thrust, Meltem spread her arms. Bone's hands padded down her field jacket.

"Hello, hello, hello, what have we here?"

Desdemona's eyes throbbed with disgust: she had an intense hatred of women human beings, and the thought of having to search one was almost as awful as the thought of having to spend the rest of her lifetime with Bone.

"*Quaaaooo*," came a faint snort from the other side of the disc.

"Bone, have some mercy! Let us free Brenda, and you—"

"SHUT THAT PLATITUDINOUS HOLE OF YOURS!" screamed the fat man. He returned his attention to the pockets inside Meltem's field jacket, from which he withdrew her small black pistol, her mobile phone and a strong but diminutive set of handcuffs.

"Strange paraphernalia for a young woman to be carrying," he gloated. "But then again, I gave up trying to understand the modern world many years ago." He shoved Meltem's belongings into the pocket of his plus-fours trousers and, with a delicate gesture, smoothed down her jacket and ran his grubby index finger fleetingly under the bottom of her chin.

Meltem shuddered but said nothing.

"Captain Bone," implored Jim in his most respectful of tones, "I'm begging you: please go and leave us. I give you my word as an archaeologist and a gentleman that we will not disclose anything about what has taken place in here. Not to anyone – neither to the Old Relics Society nor the Antiquities Squad. I promise you. Just go, please, and let us help our companion!"

"*Quaaaaoooo.*" Brenda's snort was barely audible this time.

"All righty then," smiled the fleshy man. "Desdemona and I shall be on our glorious way."

Doris's beak dropped open in disbelief.

"Thank you," said Cairo Jim. "I never thought you were *totally* evil. From one archaeologist to another, thank—"

"AND ALL THINGS ARE BRIGHT AND BEAUTIFUL," Bone shouted into Cairo Jim's face. "Oh, yes, we're going, all right. But we're taking you and the macaw and this bold little Turkish beauty with us."

"You tell 'em," croaked Desdemona, shifting her stance under the weight of the Splatto Miniature Cannon.

Bone took the handcuffs from his pocket and cuffed Jim's left wrist and Meltem's right wrist together. "Yes, you're coming along to watch what I am about to achieve. To see how I shall alter everything that has come before. To witness my new power as Lord of all the Seasons, Banisher of the Bounteous, and Baron of the Barren!"

"Rark! You're insane, you overblown great—"

"ENSHUT IT, DOLLY!" bellowed Bone. "Enough of this chit-chat. Go on, get moving." He shoved them fiercely up the sloping floor. "And, Dolly, don't even think of flying away to fetch the Antiquities Squad. Our Splatto, and my new revolver here" – he patted his trousers tenderly – "will blow your friends to Kingdom Come, a little prematurely, that's all."

"But, Brenda—" began Jim.

"MOVE!" Bone pushed them savagely up the floor.

Jim tried to turn, as they were nearing the bend in the passageway that would lead them eventually to the outside world. He tried to take a final look at the disc below. But Bone prevented him by blocking his view.

As they turned the corner and went out of the passageway, all Jim and Doris heard was a last, quiet, lingering snort.

"Quuuuuaaaaooooo?"

As the Bugatti sped along the road leading to the mountains, Cairo Jim noticed the dark, heavy clouds congregating over the distant peaks. But they were nothing compared to how dark his heart felt.

Meltem gripped his hand tightly, to try and calm him, and Doris sat in his lap, silent and fretting. Jim couldn't stand being in the power of the heinous man in the front seat, and having to leave Brenda back there, scrunched against the wall by the disc, made him feel totally helpless. His heart was being torn apart by a dreadful mixture of grief, fear and uselessness.

He felt as empty as a human being could. He breathed deeply, trying to avert the tears that were falling deep inside him from coming to the surface.

Bone had been boasting ever since they had left Kaymaklı.

"...and naturally I was destined for this above all. Desdemona, read the bit to them about what will happen when I put on the Petticoat and the Belt and the Buckle."

The raven, perched on the top of the front passenger seat, turned to Jim, Doris and Meltem. She hoisted up *At the End of the Deities* and plonked it on the top of the seat. Then she flicked through the pages impatiently with her beak.

"Crark. Listen up, losers:

"Whomsoever is able to obtain the Sacred Petticoat of Artemis, along with the Belt of Bountaiety and the Buckle of Abundance, and whomsoever is able to wear all three relics simultaneously, shall utter their own Desiderata. All powers of Nature and Abundance, yea, all the powers of Artemis Herself, will then come to such a person."

She looked up, her eyes throbbing fiendishly.

"How do you like them apples?" sneered Bone, his Belch of Brouhaha cigar sticking straight out from his flabby lips. "I don't need to remind you, but I shall, anyway – it is always satisfying to rub these things in: I have the Petticoat, safely locked in the casket in the trunk of this car. I have the Belt. I have the Buckle. I HAVE THE POWER! *Arrrrr!*"

Those in the back seat said nothing.

"And of course," Bone continued, "if I can make things fertile, then I'm willing to bet that I can *reverse* the order. To make everything as worthless as dust."

Doris could stand it no longer. "So where are you taking us?" she squawked angrily.

"To Mount Ararat," he boomed, as the road began to rise up into the mountains, and the Bugatti began its bumpy ascent.

20

THE ROAD AHEAD

BRENDA WAS WEAK and exhausted.

For many hours she had been squashed, her humps wedged hard against the huge disc and her neck and snout packed firmly against the wall. She had long given up squirming, because she found that she could barely move a millimetre, and whenever she did move even an eyelash she became more and more uncomfortable.

Panic had run through her body – a fast, desperate panic that she had never felt before. It had drained her of her Wonder Camel spirit, and now she felt limp and unclever and something else she had never felt: *doomed.*

For the first time in her life, Brenda the Wonder Camel had no hope.

She didn't know how the end would happen. She wasn't certain whether an earth tremor or a major earthquake would dislodge the floor and send the disc... She didn't want to think about *that.* Or whether there would be no earth movement, and she would be left here, alone, for days and weeks and months, until she finally... No, she didn't want to think about *that*, either.

She shut her eyelids and tried to think about their campsite, back in the Valley of the Kings. She pictured Jim's much-patched tent, and Doris's perch and Shakespeare lectern, and her own favourite bit of sand and her sandcarpet. She thought about her stash of Melodious Tex western adventure novels, and how she would never be able to read another one again. A large tear dropped from her left eye, and she snorted quietly.

And then her ears pricked up sharply, rubbing hard against the wall.

There had been a noise!

She listened hard. Now there was silence, still and awful, so quiet it was almost ringing in her ears. Then—

The noise came again!

Sssccchhhhhhhrrrrrrrkkkkkkkkkkkkkk!

And then more silence.

Brenda's heart beat like there was a tornado in her ribcage. The noise had come from below, from under the stone floor.

SSSccchhhhhhhrrrrrrrkkkkkkkkkkkkkk!

Again it came, grinding along under the stone. Through her trembling eyelids, Brenda looked up the wall against which she was wedged. The top of it, where it met the ceiling, was moving.

A tidal wave of fear swept through Brenda's body: *another earthquake!* No! Now the disc would—

SSSCCCChhhhhhhrrrrrrrkkkkkkkkkkkkkk!

She looked down, down between her huddled knees, to the floor and, as she did so, she felt herself rising. Her humps moved slowly up, rubbing against the tread of the disc.

SSSCCCCHHHHHHHrrrrrrrkkkkkkkkkkkkk!

The noise was louder now, coming closer, moving directly under her. She felt her flanks dripping with a sudden outpouring of sweat, and her nostrils flared wildly as she rose higher and higher.

The floor under her was splitting, being torn asunder with a monstrous ripping of rock.

SSSCCCCHHHHHHHRRRRRRR-kkk-kkk-kkk-kkk-k!

Small bits of rock fell from the ceiling. Now the disc began to rise as well, up and up and up, all the way to the ceiling.

SSSCCCCHHHHHHHHRRRRRRR-KKK-KKK-KKK-KKKK!

"Quaaaooooooo!" Brenda snorted, wildly, terrifyingly, beginning to despair.

There below, visible through the great cracks in the floor, was a shimmering, moving mass of colours. Purple and green, glistening, clammy-looking.

And a low, guttural hissing swamped the city of Kaymaklı.

"It's you," Brenda thought wildly. "You've come back!"

The huge head of the Belligerent Serpent of Antiocheia erupted through the floor, sliding up against the part of the wall where Brenda had been wedged. Its dark eyes opened and saw Brenda, and gave a flash of reassurance.

"Fear never," the Serpent intimated with the hiss of a thousand steaming kettles. "Thisssss place isssss but a temporary dwelling."

"Quaaooo." Brenda noticed something new about the Serpent; something that had not been before. Now, all along the Serpent's scales, there sprouted small leaves and twigs and tiny branches. A row of soft ferns hung from the many wrinkles above its eyes.

"Be ssssstill, protector of the passssst," the Serpent told Brenda by way of a mighty hiss.

Brenda didn't move a muscle.

With a huge flick of its tail, the Belligerent Serpent of Antiocheia broke through the floor beneath the disc. The disc rose high into the air, then came down with a *crash* onto the now-elevated floor, well away from Brenda's humps, and rolled off along the newly made slope – back in the direction from where it had come.

The Serpent waited until the disc had disappeared down the passageway. Brenda heard a loud noise as the disc crashed onto its side in one of the wider places back towards the entrance.

Then the Serpent flicked its leafy, scaly head, and its forked tongue licked the air. "You mussssst follow me," came its gentle, loud hissing. "I know where your friendsssss are. You must ssssstop the wrong that isssss about to happen."

"Quaaaooo."

"Follow," hissed the Serpent. "I will be all-under, all-going, all-pressssssent. Follow the ripplesssss in the floor within thisssss city, for they will be me guiding you. Asssss I will guide you on the roadway outssssssside."

The Serpent looked at Brenda, its eyes dark and timeless. With a slither and a flick, it shot down under the cracks, and Brenda watched it as it buckled the floor ahead.

21
KNOWING NO BOUNDS

THE MOUNTAINOUS AIR of Ararat was cold and bitter.

The Bugatti climbed the steep dirt road, juddering as it passed over deep potholes, its gears grinding and wrenching as Bone negotiated the curves ahead.

Gradually, as the vehicle moved higher up the mountainside, the snow-capped peaks on all the surrounding mountains began to appear, like gigantic, pointed, iced cakes towering around the tiny car.

"We'll go as high as the road will take us," Bone called over his shoulder. "I want you all to have the very best vantage point possible, so that you may view the last great spectacle of your miserable, wretched little lives."

"You're never going to see the light of day after this," Meltem seethed at him.

"Oh, hardy-ha-haaaarrrrrr," sneered Bone.

"Nevermore, nevermore, nevermore to you three," croaked Desdemona.

Jim and Doris were tormented by the thought of their Bactrian friend and what Bone had done to her.

Soon the road came to a grassy verge, and Bone steered the Bugatti onto it. He threw open his door and went to the edge. "Yes," he said to himself. "Yes, yes,

yes. This is as good a place as any." He rotated on his plump heel and addressed his captives. "Here is the spot where you shall behold the only miracle you are ever going to witness. Desdemona, open their door."

"Aye, aye, my Captain." She hopped to the door handle and flipped it upwards.

"Come to me," Bone said, in the sort of voice that suggested he were a great god.

Doris hop-fluttered onto Jim's pith helmet. Jim and Meltem, still handcuffed, climbed out of the car and strode over to Bone.

"Now open the trunk," Bone commanded the raven.

She hopped over the seat and down along the back of the car to the trunk. With a quick clunk of her beak on the handle, the trunk flew open, throwing her up into the air.

Bone put his arm around Meltem, and turned her so that she and Jim were facing the mountainscape and all that lay below. "See?" he purred. "All that land down there. One hundred and fifty thousand square kilometres, all of it as barren and infertile as a wart."

"So?" said Jim, the fury in his voice making Meltem jump. "So what?"

"It's all *mine*, that's so what! Every single nanomillimetre! I have the deeds to prove it, all legal – what a dreadful word *that* is – and proper. All that land you see before you is about to become the canvas for the greatest bout of Genius that has ever been."

"You mean—?" stammered Doris.

"Yes, bossy-beak, I shall make it all fertile, green and bounteous. Then I shall sell every bit of land down there for a vast and tidy profit. And then, after it has all been bought, I shall *revert* Nature, and make the land worthless and dry again. And buy it all back for an even *vaster* profit. Then I'll make it green and sell it again, all for my profit, ever-growing, ever fatter."

"You should know about that," Doris scowled.

"But I shall not cease there. Oh, heavens to the Goddess Betsy, no. There are deserts out there, great sandy places that I shall buy with my newly found wealth. And I shall turn them into lush and verdant paradises to sell and make *more* money! Then I shall change them back into sandy wastelands again, and buy them back for next-to-nothing, and so the process goes on and on and gloriously on."

"The world isn't big enough for such greed!" said Cairo Jim.

"In this way, I will soon *own* the world! But let us do, rather than speak!" Bone's eyes were ablaze with immense possibilities. "First, though, I think we should experiment on a smaller scale, do you think not?"

He strode to the trunk of the Bugatti and took out the egg-trimmed casket. Ripping open the lid, he withdrew the long, trailing, bulbously pleated Sacred Petticoat of Artemis and held it in front of his wide girth.

The Petticoat shimmered and glowed with a light that was unnatural.

Jim gasped. "The garment itself!"

"Rark! It's sublime!"

Meltem's eyes filled with the incandescent sight of the apparel.

Above, the clouds continued to roll in, heavy and dark, laden with great weight.

"Desdemona, get me a twig. Old and dead. The deadest you can find!"

"Aye, aye!" She flew off into the scrub by the side of the road.

Bone held the Petticoat high above his head. With a wriggle, he slithered it down over his body, pulling it and teasing, until his head popped out through the neck opening, and the hem of the Petticoat brushed against the ground. The embroidered shapes of round, plump fruits stuck out from his belly like overfilled balloons.

"Now for the final touches," he gloated. With a fluid motion, his pudgy hands threaded the Buckle of Abundance onto the Belt of Bountaiety and slid it to one end. Then he wrapped the great gold-and-silver belt around the waist of the Petticoat and did up the Buckle.

Cairo Jim's blood chilled as he beheld the gross and ruthless man adorned with such ancient importance.

Bone shut his eyes, then opened them again. "Arrr, I can almost feel the power of Nature rippling through my flesh," he leered.

"That'd be an awful lot of rippling," said Doris.

Before Bone could reply, Desdemona flew back with a small, gnarled twig in her beak. She spat it at the hem of the Petticoat and looked up at Bone. "Women's clothing *again*?" she muttered mockingly.

"Enshut thyself, Desdemona. Give me the twig at once!"

She picked up the twig in her beak and hovered up to his shoulder height. He reached out and grabbed it.

"Behold," he said to Jim, Doris and Meltem. "Behold the very first of the Modern-Day Miracles of Artemis!"

And, holding the twig close to his lips, he muttered his Desiderata earnestly at it.

Ahead, the highway stretched towards the mountains.

Brenda galloped along with the wings of a thousand ancient whispers powering her hoofs. She kept her eyes opened wide so that she could follow her guide: the dusty surface of the road, which rippled here and buckled there, all the time advancing and pulsating, as the Belligerent Serpent of Antiocheia surged forwards under the ground.

Even with her gaze fixed firmly on the roadway, Brenda could still sense the enormous, black, fulminous clouds gathering above the mountaintops...

Bone held the twig in his trembling hands.

He squinted at it with his beady eye. He turned it over and over again. He held it up against the sky, so that its bony-whiteness was stark against the dark clouds.

"It should have changed," he frowned. "By now it

should have leaves sprouting from it, and the wood should be all new and fresh!"

"I knew it," said Desdemona. "I knew this was all too far-fetched to be true!"

Jim whispered quickly to Meltem and Doris: "There's one thing he's forgotten."

"I can't understand it," said Bone, scratching his beard. "I've done everything by the book. I've followed all the instructions according to the legends in *At the End of the Deities*. Why doesn't it happen?"

Desdemona flew into the car and flicked through the old book. After a few moments, she thumped the pages savagely with her beak and raised her throbbing eyes. "Here's why, you great lump of lingerie. It says in here that 'She who wore the Petticoat of Artemis, around which was buckled the gold-and-silver Belt of Bountaiety, would have untold powers of fruitfulness.' *She.* She, she, she!"

"You mean?" Bone shot her a glare.

"Yep," grimaced Desdemona. "I never thought I'd hear meself say it, but we need a woman!"

Bone's head shot around and his razor-like gaze came to rest on Meltem Bottnoff. "Arrr, we have one at our very disposal. Madam, your hour has come!"

"No!" shouted Meltem.

"Leave her alone!" Jim bellowed.

"You, sir, are hardly in a position to remonstrate. So shut thy exclamation-hole."

Steady rumbles came from the clouds as Bone

un-handcuffed Meltem and separated her from Jim before cuffing Jim and Doris together, lacing the cuffs around a branch of a nearby tree.

In little more than a minute, Meltem was plunged into the Sacred Petticoat of Artemis, and the Belt of Bountaiety was buckled about her slender waist.

"Now, madam," Bone hissed, holding the twig against her cheek, "say 'Desiderata' three times and wish for this twig to come to life again. Quickly!"

"Never," said Meltem, her chin thrust out.

Bone took the small pistol from his plus-fours, and aimed it at Jim and Doris. "Say it, and wish it, or your pals get it!"

Meltem looked at the pistol, then at Jim and Doris. Her eyes saw Jim, and her heart saw him, and she knew she would do anything to keep him in this world.

She shut her eyes, and obeyed Bone's instructions, whispering quietly and reluctantly.

The clouds above stopped rumbling. They stilled, staying silently where they were.

Bone held the twig up against the sky...

...and slowly, tenderly, like wisps of air, the twig burst forth with new green shoots.

The shoots grew and grew, enlarging and filling, becoming healthy, lustrous, glistening leaves. With a shifting of texture, the old, wizened wood of the twig had become fresh and green.

"Crack my crest," gasped Doris.

"Pickle me eyeballs," Desdemona croaked.

"It works!" Bone shrieked with joy. "It is mine, this power of the heavens, this harnessing of Nature!"

Jim looked away. He saw the clouds starting to move again, but this time with a swiftness and silent ferocity that he had never before seen.

Bone spun Meltem fiercely around and looked deeply into her eyes. "Now listen, madam: do what you just did again, but this time concentrate your Desiderata upon the 150,000 square kilometres below. Make it fertile, make it as green as this twig, all over! Do it! Do it now!"

A swift gust of wind rose over the mountaintops, blowing firmly against the clearing. It whipped up dead leaves and clouds of dust and swirled them all about.

"Rerark!" screeched Doris as her feathers started being wildly buffeted in all directions.

Now Brenda was following the cracking, buckling roadway higher and higher up Mount Ararat.

She felt the chill of the mountain air rushing through her body. She watched the path of the Serpent. She saw the darkness growing and growing as the clouds thickened and swelled. She heard, through her Wonder Camel ears, the rumbling thunder building from somewhere far away...

"Do it, I say! Obey me, madam, or I'll blast a neat hole into your pal, before you can say 'Constantinople'!"

Meltem Bottnoff, Senior Retriever of Ancientness

with the Istanbul Branch of the Antiquities Squad, gulped deeply. She looked far out, scanning the thousands of hectares of land below – all of it dry and rocky, every part of it without any healthy vegetation. She saw the boulders and the dried-up river beds and the withered trees and straggly shrubs. She felt the great weight of the ancient Petticoat being billowed by the wind, and the gold-and-silver Belt and Buckle hanging heavily around her. She shuddered at her predicament.

With a deep breath, she whispered the Desiderata three times into the wind. And wished for fruitfulness on the land below.

"Bone!" screamed Jim, above the rumbling and the gale, "in the name of all things natural, no! Stop this! You don't know what you unleash when you mess with the past like this!"

Neptune Flannelbottom Bone ignored Jim's outburst, and concentrated on the landscape that was his.

"Crark!" Desdemona croaked. "Look! It's raining out there!"

Bone's eyes glinted with pleasure.

All above the 150,000 square kilometres, the dark clouds had opened, and a steady, heavy rainfall was pouring down. It swept across the land, back and forth, north and south, eastwards and westwards, as the winds carried the water over every valley and plain.

And then, as everyone watched from above, the land began to change: the water in the riverbeds began, slowly and steadily, to flow; the dirty, scrubby earth

started to turn green as shoots of lush, thick grass emerged. The trees bent and rose again, no longer dead and dusty, but green and new, with fresh branches growing at an astonishing rate.

The rain eased gradually, and flowers started to appear: poppies, dotting the greenery with their blood-red spots, chamomile and lavender, hyacinths, wild roses and sage. The land was carpeted with blooms.

Full, plump apples appeared on the trees, as well as oranges, peaches and nectarines. Despite the darkness from the clouds, the land below was bright with colour.

Bone was almost beside himself with pleasure. "Arrrr! Arrrr! *Arrrrr!* It works! The power of Artemis is MINE!"

"Bone!" Jim yelled. "Stop now, before—"

Bone grabbed Meltem's shoulders and pressed his bulbous nose close to hers. "Now, madam, turn it BACK!"

"Reeerrraaaaarrrk!" screeched Doris. "You mustn't!"

"No," Meltem said, trying to pull away from him. "It's going against Nature!"

"Do it," Bone seethed at her. "Unless you want to see *them* over by the tree, deady-bones!"

"I won't," Meltem said. "You haven't the nerve to shoot them, you great cowardly usurper!"

"Oh, no? Watch this, Miss Petulance!"

He raised the pistol and pointed it at the head

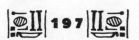

of Cairo Jim. "How I've waited for this moment," he whispered into the thunderous wind.

"*QUUUAAAAAAAOOOOOOOOO!*" A fierce snort lashed out above the rumbling and the turbulence. There, turning up the rise, was Brenda, coming full-on at the gallop!

"Halt, you deranged beast!" shouted Bone, but Brenda rushed ahead until she was between him and Jim and Doris. With a skidding of her hoofs, she halted and glared balefully at him, her nostrils blasting.

"I'm sure we have enough bullets for one more," he snarled, adjusting his aim so it was straight at her snout. "Life is sweet sometimes, is it not?"

And, closing one eye, Neptune Bone shot at Brenda.

"*NO!*" Cairo Jim's desperate cry exploded into the winds.

22

A BLAST FROM THE PAST

IN THE NANOSECOND that Bone's fat finger squeezed the trigger, the elements made their mark.

A savage bolt of lightning shot down from the fuming clouds and speared brilliantly towards the earth.

Cccchchhhhhhhhhhrrrrrrrnnnnkkkkkk!

The bullet that was travelling directly to Brenda's head was blasted clean-through by the lightning bolt and was dashed to the ground.

"What in the name of Edison?" shrieked Bone.

"Brenda, my lovely!" bellowed Jim. "Over here, behind the tree, before he fires again!"

"Arrrrrr!" Bone's beard bristled with fury, and his eyes flashed more venomously than a thousand snakes'. "You can't escape me, for I have the power!"

He raised the pistol again and followed Brenda around the tree. Like a fatty panther, he sprang in front of her. "So long, camel-breath!"

Just as he was about to squeeze the trigger again, another bolt of lightning shot down, scorching the dirt directly in front of him. At the same time, a series of bolts speared down – all around Bone – forming a cage of lightning, ripping through the sound barrier and searing the earth.

CCCChchhhhhhhhhhrrrrrrnnnnkkkkkk!
CCCCHCHHHHHHHHHHrrrrrrnnnnkkkkkk!
CCCCHCHHHHHHHHHHrrrrrr-nnnn-kkkkkk!
CCCCHCHHHHHHHHHHRRRRRR-nnnn-kkkkkk!
CCCCHCHHHHHHHHHHRRRRRR-NNNN-
Kkkkkk!

"*Oooooooooaaaaaaarrrrrrr!*" he screamed. He turned to run, but the lightning did not stop – whenever one bolt burnt away, another slammed down, then another and another, all of them encircling him in a fiery, blinding booth of electrical fire.

"*Craaarrrrkkk!*" Desdemona's eyeballs throbbed painfully, and all of her fleas bit savagely at the sound of the strikes. "I'm outta here! This ain't no place for a raven of my sensitivities!" She raised her wings and took off, buffeted wildly about by the force of the winds.

"Help!" wailed Bone. Wherever he turned, a new bolt of lightning zapped down, sealing his imprisonment. "No! I'm too young to be burnt to a crisp! *Heeeeelpppppppppppp!*"

CCCCHCHHHHHHHHHHRRRRRR-NNNN-
KKKKKK!

Meltem slipped away to the tree. She reached into her jacket pocket, underneath the Petticoat, and took out the key to the handcuffs. "Quickly," she urged as she struggled to undo the lock binding Jim and Doris together.

CCCCHCHHHHHHHHHHRRRRRR-NNNN-
KKKKKK!

CCCCHCHHHHHHHHHHHRRRRRR-NNNN-KKKKKK!

CCCCHCHHHHHHHHHHHRRRRRR-NNNN-KKKKKK!

The lightning continued to spear down, trapping Bone like a terrified animal. "ARRRRRR! It's getting closer! It'll have my toes in a—"

"Jim!" screamed Meltem.

Jim and Doris, busy with getting the handcuffs off, turned to see Meltem being drawn away by the wind. She was being pulled backwards, the Sacred Petticoat of Artemis billowing around her so that she was barely visible inside it.

"Rark!" Doris cried. "She's being pulled to the edge of the cliff!"

"Quaaaoooo!" Brenda gave a huge snort, and went to help Meltem, but it was useless: the wind was too strong – almost cyclone force now – and it drove the Wonder Camel sharply back against the tree.

"Help me!" Meltem shouted, her chin sticking out bravely but with terror in her eyes.

"Help *me*!" Bone screamed, still trapped in the cage of lightning bolts.

"Meltem!" shouted Jim, as she was pulled closer and closer to the very edge of the cliff. Below was a drop of at least three thousand metres, all of it straight down.

"Jim!" Meltem cried, her eyes wild, big, dark, as she was being dragged further and further away from him. She reached out, her fingers stretching against the gale, but it was no good – she was almost on the very precipice, and she could feel the gravity behind her clawing at the back of the Petticoat, trying to pull her over and down...

"Take off the Belt!" Jim yelled.

"What?"

"The Belt of Bountaiety! Take it off! Then you won't have the combination of relics any more!"

The wind ripped all around them, and the lightning speared at Bone.

CCCCHCHHHHHHHHHHHRRRRRR-NNNN-KKKKKK!

CCCCHCHHHHHHHHHHHRRRRRR-NNNN-KKKKKK!

CCCCHCHHHHHHHHHHHRRRRRR-NNNN-KKKKKK!

"I can't hear you!" Meltem yelled, the Petticoat whipping her from sight. "Jim, I'm about to—" She felt her heels sliding back, down, into nothing.

"No you don't!" thought Jim.

Where it came from, he knew not, but Cairo Jim found a break in the wind and a burst of over-reaching strength, and he leapt at Meltem, grabbing her shoulders and pulling her back towards him. In the next second he ripped the Belt of Bountaiety and the Buckle of Abundance from around her waist, and flung them into the skies.

The wind rose further, picking up the gold-and-silver Belt and Buckle, and whooshing them through the air. Up and up they rose, wildly flapping into the clouds.

There was the loudest rumbling in 2000 years as the clouds in the centre of the sky parted.

Jim, Doris, Brenda and Meltem watched as the Belt and Buckle glinted against the lightning and then disappeared above the clouds.

CCCCHCHHHHHHHHHHHRRRRRR-NNNNNN-KKKKKK!

A final, fierce battalion of lightning bolts hurtled down around Bone's feet, singeing his spats and hurling him high into the air. He landed with a heavy *thlummmp*.

"Arrrr, arrrrr, I'm off. Blow this for a career!"

He rolled over, sprang up, and jumped into the Bugatti. He started the engine and sped off down the mountain road.

"I'll get you, Jim, and when I do you'll wish you'd never been born! ARRRRRRRRRRRR..."

"*Raaark*," screeched Doris. "After him!"

"No," said Jim. "Look! Something strange..."

The lightning stopped. The rumbling of the thunder subsided. The clouds began to disperse, slinking away quickly and wispily.

Sunshine emerged, bathing the rich, green land in a soft and gentle glow.

"Quaaaaaoooo," snorted Brenda, looking up.

Jim noticed her eyes scanning the heavens. He, Doris and Meltem looked up as well.

There, silhouetted in the last of the heavy clouds, was the image of a face, rolling and shifting: a strong yet delicate jaw, setting off high cheekbones; a pair

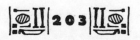

of commanding eyes; a kindly smile on soft and gentle cloud-lips.

"Artemis," Jim whispered.

"Like the statue," cooed Doris.

Meltem trembled and brushed her hair from her eyes.

"Quaaaoooo," snorted Brenda, raising her head high at the cloud formation.

With a final wafting of an ancient breeze, the clouds dispersed and drifted away into the ether. Artemis had come for what was hers, and now She was gone forever.

Two days later, back at the Istanbul headquarters of the Antiquities Squad, Jim, Doris and Brenda said goodbye to Meltem Bottnoff.

"I shall have the Petticoat delivered to the Archaeological Museum this afternoon," she told them.

"To be exhibited under lock and key," smiled Jim.

"Under lock and key," she smiled back.

"Rerark! Let's go, Jim. I want to get back home!" Doris flexed her gold-and-blue wings impatiently. "Goodbye, Meltem Bottnoff. It was an experience I shall never forget."

Meltem tousled Doris's crestfeathers. "Goodbye, Doris. Thank you."

"Quaaooooooo," farewelled Brenda, fluttering her beautiful eyelashes.

"Farewell, Brenda," said Meltem, rubbing the Wonder Camel's mane gently.

Jim put on his special desert sun-spectacles and his pith helmet. "Thank you, Meltem. It's good to know the Antiquities Squad has such professional and reliable people in its midst."

He extended his hand to her, and it enveloped her smaller hand.

"Jim," she said, gazing at her reflection in his sun-spectacles. "I wonder ... would there be any chance of us meeting again?"

Her hand remained in his, but for Meltem the seconds would never be long enough.

"Who knows?" he answered. "The world's a big place, with all sorts of things going on. And, in our work, it's quite possible that History, and all that it conceals, will bring us together again."

"Yes," she said quietly. "One of those little, forgotten pockets..."

He smiled, and withdrew his hand. "Goodbye, Meltem. I'll tell my friend Jocelyn all about you."

"Goodbye, Jim." Then, without even planning to, she reached up and kissed him lightly on the cheek.

The archaeologist-poet blushed.

"Here we go," Doris squawked, rolling her eyes.

Jim and Doris mounted Brenda's saddle, and Meltem watched the three head out of the office building and along the sokak.

She stayed at the entrance to the building for a

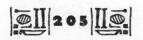

long time after they had left, not seeing the street or hearing the horns of the cars, or even noticing the light creeping into the evening.

Then, when darkness had fully arrived, she sighed, took a deep breath, and went inside to tend to her ailing saxifraga plant.

▲▲▲▲▲ EPILOGUE ▲▲▲▲▲

FOUR MONTHS LATER, a young shepherd was tending his sheep one afternoon in the lush countryside near Mount Ararat.

He was walking through the flock, thinking how remarkable the change in the land around these parts had been, when he stubbed his toe on something half-sticking out of the earth.

Bending down, he uncovered what looked like a large belt. He pulled it from the ground and carefully began wiping the caked-on dirt from it.

It was pretty, he decided, when he had got most of the dirt and grime off. It would look very good around his favourite sheep, a large and bossy animal named Selma.

He beckoned Selma over to him, and lovingly fastened the tarnished but beautiful object around her middle. She looked up at him, then at her new waistband, then at him again.

"Because you are the Queen of the World," he said, rubbing her ear.

"Baaaaaaaaaaaa!" she bleated loudly, before marching off to display herself proudly to all her woolly friends.

THE END

Swoggle me sideways!

Unearth more thrilling mysteries
of history starring Cairo Jim, Doris,
and Brenda the Wonder Camel –

THE CAIRO JIM
CHRONICLES

The Cairo Jim Chronicles,
read by Geoffrey McSkimming,
are available on CD
from Bolinda Audio Books!
See **www.bolinda.com** for details.